C000157229

The Man for the Job

The Man for the Job

Laurie Graham

Chatto & Windus London

Published in 1986 by
Chatto & Windus Ltd
40 William IV Street
London WC2N 4DF

All rights reserved. No part of this publication may be
reproduced, stored in a retrieval system, or
transmitted in any form, or by any means, electronic,
mechanical, photocopying, recording or otherwise,
without the prior permission of the publisher.

British Library Cataloguing in Publication Data
Graham, Laurie
  The man for the job.
  I. Title
  823'.914[F]   PR6057.R23/

  ISBN 0–7011–3981–1

Copyright © Laurie Graham 1986

Typeset at The Spartan Press Ltd
Lymington, Hants
Printed in Great Britain by
Redwood Burn Ltd
Trowbridge, Wiltshire

Chapter 1

The detestable month of August had gone. On its last tide it had quietly restored Daddo's health and left the shops full of geometry sets. Money was tight. Spending cuts deep. And the school-leaving age had been upped to nineteen. Didge braced himself for Life Experience Studies with the Easter Leavers and had the humility to admit that he was cycling towards the lowpoint of his teaching career.

He made good time so as to have the luxury of the longer way in and avoid the weapons check at the main gate. It was good to be out.

He laid his bike gently on its side in the long grass that edged the playing field and sat down to watch. Amble and Lull were nearing the staff entrance, earnestly shaggy, comparing espadrilles. Gaining on them fast, lunchbox in one hand, truncheon in the other, was Boyle. He was a welcome sight. Didge thought he'd gone. He'd been promoted to good prospects and the Maximum Security Reading Difficulties Unit. They'd had a whip-round, bought him a new bull-worker, and he'd gone. But he was back. Large as life and twice as nasty, back at Freshfields where he was needed.

He was the only man who could be relied upon to appear when the Panic Bell rang. The only one who knew for sure how to inflict pain and leave no tell-tale marks. Boyle promised survival. And uneasy security. Like sleeping with a Dobermann. As if he read Didge's thoughts he waggled his weapon at Donna as he overtook her pushing a child in a striped pushchair. Or was it Zoë Claire? Whichever it was, it was noticeably pregnant again.

1

This was quite beyond Didge. Twenty years amongst the lower animals had allowed him to grasp the scale of their intellect. He had learned to make some sense of their rudimentary language, and how to dodge their blows. But the ease with which they reproduced themselves utterly defeated him.

He had never done the thing himself. He knew from the changing-room of life that he had the equipment, and he had gathered from certain consequences of watching a French film in which a woman took off her blouse, that it was in working order. But he also knew a thing or two about sticklebacks and pollen. He knew that it took motivation, co-ordination, and a following wind. He knew that Zoë Claire would have had none of these. Or was it Donna? He freed his underpants from the crack of his behind and set off towards school.

Inside there was no air. The kept and the keepers were at it already, outwitting, being outwitted. In the Staff Refuge escape plans were in an advanced state of readiness, and in the Technical Studies No-Go Area a counterplot was well in hand. Some stood in nervous grazing herds ready to bolt at the first whiff of trouble. And others kept on the move, pretending they had important business. Only one man knew exactly where he was going and what he was going to do when he got there. Swills.

The crowds parted for him as he passed, small and strong, with a pail of bleach and a squeegee. He spoke as he went, indifferent to his audience. He took his words with him through many time zones, and those who heard his opening remarks had to make enquiries about his conclusions. Swills spoke for his own satisfaction.

'They're at it again. It's started.'

And indeed it had. All around old customs were being revived. Scuffles had broken out, slowly at first like half-remembered dance steps, and then with confidence, and the shedding of blood. Celia Corrigan was calling to be let out of

2

the music-room. And in the Third Year cloak-room Natasha and Elaine were taking bookings for tattoos. The first thing to do was to get through to the office. Find out which room. Get a class list. Learn the worst.

Colin Cherish had hesitant possession of his own study doorway. He wanted to disappear behind it but he knew he should be brave, so he hovered, fingering his Snap-Bak safety tie and apologising to those who stood on him. He spotted Didge and saw his chance. They might be going to have a long and futile argument about teaching schedules. Didge might break down and weep when he read his student allocations. It should happen discreetly. Behind closed doors. Cherish embraced Didge warmly.

'My dear, dear Filbert!'

'Headmaster!'

'Come in. Come in. First day. Chaos reigns. Good holidays?'

'Quiet, Headmaster. Very quiet.'

'Jolly good. The best sort, dear boy.'

'And you, Headmaster?'

'Scotland.'

'Ah yes. Mrs Cherish's . . . ?'

'Sister. Yes. Scotland. Know it at all?'

'A little.'

'We visited a whisky distillery.'

'Yes? I suppose you would. That's the trouble with the place.'

'And mountains. We stopped off at a number of mountains for coffee.'

'That's the thing about Scotland. Scenic views. Stirring music. A hateful country. Hateful.'

'Yes. We always go.'

Cherish sat down behind his desk and searched for the right pile of papers. Didge could see immediately which one it was. There was a red file. Even upside down it said Eighteen Plus

3

Remedial. That one would be his. Eventually Cherish put his hand to it.

'Ah, yes. Sit down, sit down.'

The chair that Bianca had broken over Cherish's head on the last day of term had not been replaced so Didge remained standing.

'You'll be pleased to hear we're leaving things pretty open ended for you this year.'

'Open ended?'

'Yes.'

'No timetable?'

'Not as such.'

'Is this wise?'

'Well, we are three timetable enforcement auxiliaries down on last year . . .'

'Cutbacks?'

'As you say. And the thing is, it *is* a pretty impressive class list. More than half of them are reading tolerably. And then some of them are ready for First Steps to Numeracy. You've got one or two old lags . . . Kandy, Michelle, Carly-Jayne . . . But nothing you can't manage . . .'

'But no timetable.'

'We took the view you might prefer to . . .'

'Improvise?'

'That's it. See how it goes. Play it by ear. Find out what they really want to learn, and . . .'

'Make it fun?'

'Exactly.'

A body fell heavily against the other side of the door.

'One or two other little points. We've changed the crêche provisions.'

'Scrapped?'

'No, no. We've needed to extend for some time, and with two more arrivals since July . . . No. We've set on a full-time nursery nurse. Sole responsibility. You see there are those who

4

feel it was all a bit of a skive for the little mothers. Feeding-times and so forth. We're obliged to give them time for post-natal thingies. Required by statute. But they can learn to be parents in their own good time. I think it's for the best. Force them into the practicalities too early and child and mother may be scarred for life. Or so I was reading. We've got this nanny person now, so let her see to it all. My own mother always thought that was the best way, and we did quite nicely on it. Funny how these things come round again. The old ideas. And it will leave Donna and others with more time for their projects.'

'And probably be a great relief to Donna's child.'

'My point exactly. Free them to discover the magic of word and number, and the mothering will follow.'

It was as Didge had guessed. The ones a teacher could still get his teeth into – the young, the enterprising, the violent – they had all gone to members of staff who could put up a show of fruitless optimism. Rookies, a lot of them. Or better at pretending than he was. He had won the wooden spoon. If only he had reined in his cynicism he might have got the Second Year Psychopaths. He'd finished July looking bored and weary. And now they were phasing him out. Eighteen Plus Remedial were women. Some of them had been women for nearly ten years. What had once passed for childhood, they had packed with frantic self-destruction. Name it and they had seen it, smoked it, or disembowelled it. They had acquainted themselves with upholsterer's adhesive, intimate diseases and organised crime. And they had left till last the more difficult skills. Like learning. And self-discipline. They were push-button girls. Beaten from the start by the time scale of a thing called deferred gratification.

'And Filbert. There was one other thing . . .'

What more could there be? Less money? Longer hours? Would he have to teach them Latin? Where was it all going to end?

'Headmaster?'

'We thought we'd give you a move. I thought we'd give you a move.'

'Ah.'

'Fresh outlook. Vistas new. A change of stamping ground.'

'Ah.'

'The Annexe.'

'I see.'

'Knew you would. Years of experience. Master of your craft. Man like you could teach in a cardboard shoebox.'

'The Annexe?'

'Had it emulsioned. Pampas Green. Bags of space. Creative play and so forth.'

Didge had to work very hard at looking disappointed. The Annexe was a bonus he hadn't dreamed of. Its advantages were lost on Headmaster. He'd never set foot in the place. His agoraphobia prevented him from making the trip. But Didge knew the Annexe. It was spacious, self-contained and ripe for a little freelance improvement. Best of all it was a windswept five hundred yards from the main school building. He knew he must protest. But not too much.

'I suppose it has to fall to someone.'

'It has.'

'And I suppose as one of the longer-serving . . .'

'That was what I thought.'

'I should like my misgivings put on record.'

'Consider it done.'

'All right then. I'll give it a go.'

'That's the spirit. I know you're the man for it. Rosalind was against it, but I told her you were the man for it.'

Rosalind Strutt had very sound instincts sometimes.

Didge was quietly thankful that, as a woman, she would always be kept from power. He moved on to surer ground.

'I see Boyle is back.'

'Boyle?'

'Physical Education. With the truncheon.'

'You mean Boyle! He's back.'

'I thought he'd gone. I'm sure we collected for him.'

'Burned down. The Corby Unit for High Risk Non-Readers. Razed to the ground. Dreadful business.'

'Local residents?'

'Staff.'

'Poor Boyle. He had expectations.'

'Well . . .'

'Well. I'll take the file and beetle over to the Annexe. Take a look around.'

'That's right.'

'Nose to the grindstone.'

'Shoulder to the wheel.'

'I'll let you know.'

'Yes?'

'I'll let you know how it goes.'

'That's the spirit. Any problems, pop along and run them up the flagpole.'

Didge backed out of Headmaster's office and slid away into the silence of the Metalwork Corridor, strictly out of bounds since the Armalite incident. Two very small girls were forcing a store-room door. Otherwise this backwater was deserted.

He coaxed his sixteen stones into a modest gambol and was about to try a hop, skip and a jump, when he was stopped and cooled by the thin vibration of a familiar voice. The store-room burglars pressed on with their business. But Didge was rooted.

'Mr Didge! Mr Didge! A little help if you'd be so kind.' It was Rosalind Strutt.

Six weeks of sun had left her cheeks and her moustache untouched. She was a pale woman. Of an age that makes men anxious. Her mind was well exercised. She had been a classics scholar, beached, left high and dry by the retreat from excellence. And she showed great courage at every failed attempt to refloat her. But her body was weak. Under her cotton frock she was twisted from long hours absorbed with Saint Paul under a forty watt bulb. A clever little grub who had stayed too long in a small dark cell ever to be able to fly.

'Rosalind! Good morning!'

'Filbert!' She was breathless.

'I've just seen Headmaster. He seems well rested.'

'I saw you. I was trying to catch you.'

'Did you manage to get away?'

'Mummy had a relapse.'

'You were off to Offa's Dyke, weren't you?'

'Mummy had a relapse just as I was leaving. Another hour and I'd have been on my way. I'd never have forgiven myself if anything had happened.'

'So no Offa's Dyke?'

'The main thing is I was there when I was needed.'

'And how is she now?'

'Never better. I put her to bed and just sat with her. She kept getting out and putting her clothes on but I was determined. You have to be very firm with them. She's in Tuscany now. Recuperating. I took her to the airport yesterday. She's marvellous really . . .'

'Well I'm glad she's better.'

'Oh she's wonderful. For her age. Wonderful. Did you get away?'

'No, no. Daddo's never at his best in the summer. He has to go and lie down a lot. And, if he's in bed, then Hedley's a handful.'

'Couldn't you get him in somewhere?'

'He'd get out. He's all right at home. If he's busy he's all right. It's if he gets bored. If he sees an open window he's off. He's generally in somebody's shed and you have to go round. Looking in people's sheds. And, if they're away on holiday, you don't really like to.'

'Yes. That's one thing I will say for Mummy. She never hides.'

'Did you want something?'

'But still, they *are* marvellous for their ages. Yes. Yes, Filbert, I did. I want you to translate something for me.'

Rosalind and Didge pushed back through Small Hall. The fire bell was ringing but everyone was working on the usual assumption. On the main stairs new arrivals were unscrewing the banisters. It cheered him to see such spirit. A couple of years and that would all be gone. By fifteen they would have burned themselves out and by seventeen any sign of activity behind the eyes would be cause for medical investigation. Behind bullet-proof glass Cherish's predecessor watched anxiously. Didge had known him, but without the stolen plaque he couldn't put a name to him. He'd been a pleasant man, quite unsuited to the post. Crippled by gentleness, at Freshfields there had been no crutch strong enough to bear him. He had made a stand over the netball team not wearing knickers, and finally cracked, dropping his trousers in Leavers Assembly and inviting the Board of Governors to do the same.

'It's the top floor lavatory.'

Rosalind was warbling. Didge was eager to be off to the Annexe.

'A job for Mr Swills, by the sound of it.'

'It was Mr Swills that found it, Filbert. And I want you to see it.'

What could Swills have found that was different? Were there really novelties still to be found in the top floor lavatory? The Dead Sea Scrolls perfectly transcribed onto toilet paper? Miss Wimble walled up all summer and dead for lack of tennis?

'He tried all his magic substances and nothing will move it. I might never have seen it, if the caustic soda had worked.'

'Can't he paint it out?'

'He's fetching the paint now. I asked him to wait until you'd seen it. You'll know what it means.'

'What does it say?'

9

'I always like to follow up new words, don't you? Nothing I like better than a good old session with the dictionary. How about you?'

Didge nodded. He had learned to be cautious with Rosalind. Enthusiasm had once earned him unmanageable quantities of her green tomato chutney.

'And there are some words I'm never sure how to use.'

'Epistemic.'

'No, I can manage that one.'

'Disingenuous?'

'No, no. Pillock. I'd hesitate to use that with certainty. And turned-on. What in the world does that mean?'

She laughed. The sun was in her hair and she had Hi-Bran on her front teeth.

Swills was waiting for them at the top of the stairs with his pull-along cart of paint pots. He was a taut, bony man. His skin had been intended for someone smaller.

'I hope you've waited for us, Mr Swills.'

'I could have had it done by now.'

'But Mr Didge has kindly agreed to have a crack at translating it for us.'

'What does it say, Swills?'

'Reading things is not my job. If you want things read you'll have to take it up with management.'

'Swills! Tell what it says and save me climbing any more steps.'

'I've never held with mucky talk. Nor Mrs Swills. And that Popsicle Pink's discontinued. You're never going to match that. I'll have a go with Love That Blush but I don't hold out a lot of hope. And I know who done it.'

'Tell, Swills! Tell all.'

'It was the red-head from Five Dyslexic.'

'Jo-Jo?'

'No. She's Seven Dyslexic.'

'Gracious, doesn't time fly.'

10

'Her name's Willow.'

'She's Five Hyperactive.'

'I seen her so there's no disputing it.'

Didge pushed the swing door and called ahead,

'Anyone at home?'

Swills brought the paint cart in for safety and they huddled together, pressed for space and clean air, to see what they were all there to see. Swills pointed to it.

'Bastards.'

Rosalind was impatient.

'Well, Filbert? What do you think?'

There was no arguing against it. It had been written in Dirty Damson Hard-as-Nails, and the bottle now lay in some fluffy dyslexic pocket. Didge swivelled his head both ways in the hope of sparing Rosalind a head-on collision with life. But, whichever way he tried it, it still came out the same:

TRUTTS IS A TUNC

Chapter 2

It was the grandest of mornings. The sun made the east wind allowable and Didge was listening so closely to the hypnotic flap of his trousers that he had all but reached the Annexe when he remembered something important. He should have worn a protective helmet.

Ordinarily he didn't need to think of such things. His normal duties never brought him into contact with the more violent girls. And there were plenty of them. Boyle and Nutts were Home Office trained to handle those with special needs. Some of them were frustrated high-achievers. Or so it was said. Didge had his doubts. Some of them had been thumped too often by their parents. Most of them hadn't been thumped anything like enough. And one or two belonged to a different evolutionary chapter. They had large, poor quality brains and were infertile through too much early sex. Developmental deadenders.

But they didn't concern Didge. To move about within the school building only the simplest of precautions were necessary. Such violence as occurred was usually between girls, and members of staff who moved close to the wall and averted their eyes had nothing to fear.

But a walk to the Annexe was a different matter. The house was all that was left of the old estate. It stood, substantial and separate, demanding air and getting it. It was a house that should have been filled with robust children and wet dogs.

The path to the front door was watched. No one came unnoticed. Few got in unscathed. Because, up on the second floor, crouched by a window with the sun bouncing off her specs, Dimity Hubble was on look-out for them, alert and unpaid.

Dimity had been relieved of her duties.

She was part of the very history of Freshfields. A needlework teacher who could recall the Sixties, when a girl was glad to make a gathered skirt and call it her own work. But times had changed. The fiendish orient had flooded Kettering Market with cheap cotton, and no parent in their right mind would pay for badly matched seersucker stripes, grubby and stitched to death for three whole terms.

A few girls were into collage. And tie'n'dye. But within a year it wasn't done to be into anything, and the word redundancy was on certain lips.

Dimity was an enterprising woman. First she traded on a minor disciplinary breach. It was something and nothing. Two girls called Lisa had cannibalised a sewing machine and come up with a portable skin embroiderer.

Dimity seized on the incident and treated herself to a nervous breakdown. And the authorities were understanding. Nervous exhaustion was becoming commonplace amongst senior staff.

So the necessary papers were drawn up. But she wasn't finished. She saw that more mileage could be had out of sustained eccentricity, and on 15th April 1981 she barricaded herself into the top floor of the Annexe and declared herself a republic.

She stayed up there a whole week hurling things at every psychiatrist and ne'er-do-well clergyman who tried to coax her down. Then she stayed a month, fed and watered by a band of unruly middle-aged women who had been inspired by her act of defiance.

Her husband had taken it badly at first. She had oiled his domestic wheels for thirty years, and round about the time the clean shirts ran out he decided to speak to her very firmly.

The steam-iron that hit him on the temple was beyond

13

repair, but after half of his head had gone through purple and green to yellow, they struck up a dialogue and the matter was settled. He would see to her weekly needs in baskets to be hoisted up to the second floor, and in return be granted safe passage beneath her window and sexual relations with the housekeeper of his choice.

And that was how things stood. Hubble had taken up with a string of disreputable women – chiropodists, Sunday School Teachers. Even librarians. All of them flaunted in public. And the clean shirts never ran out. Dimity stayed put. Her perm grew out and she kept her coat on all the time. Slowly she lost touch, eating straight from the cans, sniffing her armpits without pretence. And nobody bothered about needlework anymore. Only the challenges and the empty Horlicks jars singing through the air reminded the school that she was there at all.

Didge stopped for a moment and thought. He could try making a dash for it but he knew she'd spotted him by the set of her head. She was up and scanning like an old rabbit. He'd have to use what he had to hand. So he covered the top of his head with his class file and walked, steadily so as not to excite her, holding high a grey crusty handkerchief of truce.

The outer door was swinging in the wind, and the hall was full of dust and discarded computer terminals. He kept an ear cocked for Dimity on the stairs and looked behind every door.

He found the room. There was a strong smell of paint. Ten Educonsoles with two seats to each, bolted to the floor, were arranged in the horseshoe configuration favoured by the 1982 Whalley Report on Improved Classroom Performance, and at the mouth of the horseshoe was the padded, swivel chair that was to be his. There was someone in it. There was a magnifying mirror balanced on the arm and Cher was seeing to her blackheads.

'Go!'

'Let me just do this one.'

14

'Wrong room. Out!'

'Half a tick.'

'Now!'

She did a few more and then moved.

'Great chair.'

'Out! Report to Miss Strutt. Do not return.'

Cher wiped the mirror with her sleeve and pushed past him chummily.

'All right. Keep your trousers on.'

Didge tried the chair to be sure she hadn't spoilt it and as he swung to face the window he saw her again, outside looking in.

She said, 'I shouldn't mind stopping here.'

He couldn't really hear her, so he just answered, 'Go!'

At about ten they began to arrive. Small waves of them broke disorderly under Dimity's window. Gemma had a red-faced child on one arm and a bag of disposable nappies on the other. Appalled, Didge rushed to bar the way. He jabbed at it.

'What is this?'

'It's me babby. He's called Marc. Hold him a mo.'

She dumped it on Didge. It was round and red and acrid.

'Take it away.'

'It's only a babby. It's nice. Go on. Just for a bit.'

'Out. Out! This is strictly against the rules. Take it to the crêche immediately. Or take it home to your mother.'

Mandy made a solo bid.

'He don't cry a lot. I've gave him a Woogie.' And to strengthen this argument Gemma produced the Woogie from the nappy bag and rubbed its green fur against Didge's unwilling cheek.

Outside, voices were raised. Kandy, Carly-Jayne and Nikki, latecomers, were returning Dimity's compliments.

Didge went to the window.

'Get in! Get in, you horrid girls.'

And then back to Gemma, 'Get out! Take it away. And the Woggle.'

'I shall have to do his bum first.'

'And what does that involve?'

'He's shit himself.'

Kandy and Carly-Jayne joined in and showed interest.

'A babby!'

'I'd like one of them.'

'Didge gave him a cuddle.'

'Did he? Did you, Didge? Did you hold him?'

'He did. He just gave him back.'

'You old bugger. Didge's an old bugger.'

He guessed he was losing control.

'Gemma! Get him done. There's a nursery person paid to do that sort of thing so that you can be free to learn some more words and numbers.'

'I'll just do him here. He'll get sore if I don't.'

'Gemma!'

'I'm going to have to walk all the way back again.'

'Do it.'

'I'll take him after dinner. She's a cow. That woman. She keeps them in their bouncers all morning. And she nicks their choccy.'

Michelle made a practical suggestion.

'Get an oik to fetch him.'

'If I'm fetching an oik I might as well take him myself.'

'No, no. I'll get you one. With me bleeper.'

So Gemma scraped and sponged one end while Mandy distracted it with the Woogie at the other and Michelle radio-paged one of her third-year noddies. And then they all waited.

At the start of afternoon school Didge found that the girls had been busy. Aspen had unbolted her seat and moved it so that no one would have to sit next to Terri. Terri wasn't offended by this. She accepted their prejudices.

16

It wasn't because she was dirty, though she certainly was. And it wasn't because she thieved, because they all did that. It was simply this. She had once showed signs of voluntary intellectual activity.

It had been long ago. So far back that Didge had forgotten the details. But something had whetted her appetite. Something had made her ask, and look for more. And they had never forgiven that brief orgy of discovery and enthusiasm. Nor could they be blamed. There was so little left for them to persecute. Everything that was not white and unremarkable had been repatriated or banished, and there was nothing left to satisfy that basic human drive to be vicious and irrational.

So, Terri's lapse had been inflated and embellished and the truth of it then forgotten. They remembered she was an outcast, but not why, and they short-circuited her with trivia – she had warts, she still wore leg-warmers – when the essence of it was, that her mind had been places.

So Aspen had been to work and left Terri with an Educonsole all to herself, and nothing to sit on.

The door to the empty back rooms blew open and slammed shut. And then again. Didge went to see why. In the back kitchen the window frame had been removed in one piece and the front end of Tania was on its way through, pushed from behind by Farah.

'What was wrong with the door?'

'We come in this way.'

'Everyone else used the door.'

'We never.'

'It took all morning.'

'I marked you absent. Put the window back.'

'Bet you never heard nothing.'

'Can the window be put back?'

'Easy.'

'Do it. And get to your console.'

'Didge . . .'

'Do it.'

'I'm doing it. I'm doing it.'

'Didge . . . ?'

'Yes, Tania?'

'It was a good project. Don't you think?'

'Everyone else used the door.'

'But it was a good project. It echoes in here. Don't it echo a lot, Didge?'

'It sounds like the Leisurepool when they done away with the astroturf and found all them wiggly things underneath.'

And it was while Tania and Farah were trying out the back kitchen echo that Didge's idea for improving his long stretch in the Annexe really began to take shape.

Off hand he didn't know of any jacuzzi specialists, so he unlocked the phone and prepared to wait for School Office to give him a line. But out in the Annexe there was a thing called a direct line. It hummed in his ear until he recognised it for what it was and pressed the numbers for Trader Enquiries.

He connected with a pea-brained girl. She didn't know what a jacuzzi was, but wouldn't admit it. She got him an exotic pets supplier and two medical sundries warehouses before he grew so exasperated that he shouted at her to give him a plumber and he'd take it from there.

The person at Wet Dreams was as different again. And Didge was the perfect customer. He was ignorant of the facts but committed to an idea, and best of all, he was spending someone else's money. By the end of the call, something, though he couldn't swear what, had been set in motion. He'd signed nothing of course.

The girls were noisy. He asked them what they would like to do. Some of them wanted to run across the playing-field and then run back again. Most of them wanted to do arm-wrestling. But Barbie had an idea.

'Let's do what they done in olden days.'

'And what was that, Barbie?'

18

'You know.'

'Are you going to give me some clues?'

'You know. What you done first day back.'

'Well we used to work. We used to do Geography and Woodwork.'

'No you never. My Dad told me. You never done none of that. Not first day back.'

'Come on then. We're all longing to know what your Daddy did on the first day of term.'

'It starts with Ter.'

'Something beginning with Ker that Barbie's Daddy used to do on the first day back. Anyone going to guess?'

'Ter. Not Ker. Something beginning with Ter.'

'I know. I know. My Dad done it too.'

'Lee-Anne's Daddy also done it, did it, and it begins with Ter . . .'

'Sir, sir, I know.'

'Aspen?'

'Terrifying people.'

'Could be.'

'No. Not that. Do you give up then?'

'Yes we give up.'

'Timetable!'

'What?'

'Timetable.'

'My Dad done that.'

'Anybody knows that. In olden times you drawn your timetable.'

'Didge! I know another thing they done first day.'

'Nikki?'

'Covered their books with old wallpaper.'

A hot little pain began inside Didge, and it grew, as though a great oven door had swung open. It was nostalgia. It was for the days when there had been books. And paper to cover them with. And blackboards and chalk and good hidings. He perched on the edge of Jodie's console and hugged himself.

'Shall I tell you about the old days, girls?'

And for the first time they were all silent.

'We used to wear a uniform. Like the Junior Watchdogs of St George. So when people saw us in the street they knew straight away which school we were from.'

'So they knew where to come for you? If you got in any bother?'

'That sort of thing, Jacqui. And every morning we had to go into Main Hall and stand still and quiet as statues while Headmaster spoke to us. Nobody ever threw things. We wouldn't have dared. We weren't allowed to harm even ordinary members of staff. And there were most particular rules about things like starting fires.'

'And tell us about the timetables, Didge.'

'Can we do one? Can we?'

'But what would you put on it, Lindy? You see we used to have proper lessons. Like Technical Drawing. And French. What could you write on yours?'

'We could make it up.'

'Like a project.'

'A project on olden days.'

'Can we?'

'Please, Didge. Please.'

'All right. All right. Barbie, go to Main School. Find a person called Nipley in a place called Secure Stores. You may need to ask Miss Strutt where it is because others may not know . . .'

'I know what it is.'

'And I do.'

'We know where it is, don't we?'

They all knew the closely guarded secret. Didge thought he should get one of them to show him some time.

'When you arrive there say that Mr Didge needs fifty sheets of plain paper, twenty pencils and twenty rulers, for making timetables as in the old days. If Nipley doesn't understand the

20

older person Chitty certainly will, if he's still alive. Which he may not be.'

'Tell her to get some wallpaper and some books.'

'What?'

'Wallpaper.'

'No. Stores wouldn't have anything like that. They might not have rulers . . .'

'They have. And staplers.'

'And envelopes. Millions.'

'And scissors. Bring him some scissors while you're there.'

'I don't want any scissors thank you, Gemma.'

'I do.'

'Remember, Barbie, it's for timetables. For Mr Didge. But if Miss Strutt should ask, just say it's for a project. Because you're not really supposed to know about timetables. Do you understand me, Barbie?'

'Can we go out on the field now?'

'Has the window frame been put back? Then you may go, but only – wait – only if you stay within sight of this window. And when you see Barbie coming back from Main School you're to come straight in.'

Alone, Didge thought again about the back room that lay empty. A Roman Foamy Tub would make an interesting project for the girls. They could follow each stage of its installation. Really get to grips with how it worked. Then they could use it to explore the area of fluid physics. Or as a social forum, like proper Romans. And when Rosalind eventually got wind of it they could help him formulate his defence. It could be an exercise in justification. They'd be good at that. And in the meanwhile it would improve his working conditions. Banished to this windswept exile with only a deranged dressmaker for company, he deserved a few creature comforts. He could place his orders over the telephone and wait for things to happen. There need be no Rosalind listening in,

21

breathing disapproval. Cherish would sign the bills. County would pay them. County would complain about them. Cherish would query them. And finally Rosalind would rumble him. But what had been done would not be undone. It would remain as a monument to him. And Rosalind would say that she'd told them so.

He fingered the telephone, enjoying his liberation from Rosalind. For years she had tyrannised him with cost zones, off-peak rates and a little timer that went ping. Now the world was waiting for him to call. He got out his address book and glanced at the time. It was too early for Emmett, tucked up in California. And too late for Kenny, enduring New Zealand through deep healing sleep. Bo would be working. And Njomo might still be in bed. But he wouldn't mind. He'd be glad of the surprise. Didge punched in the number for International Codex and after the tone he spoke. 'Give me the Direct Dial Code for Lagos.'

Chapter 3

He didn't linger at the end of the day. The evenings were starting to draw in and the streets were not safe.

It had begun with the Molesworth Martyrs nearly two years before. On Candlemas Eve wimmin had gathered, to light peat fires and keen for Brigit, Midwife of the Spring. Five hundred police had been mustered, some mounted, some on foot, and as darkness fell the wimmin danced with rowan branches and meditated upon the Creative Spiral. While everyone ovulated the sisters from Scotland revived the custom of Pounding the Serpent, and then the fires were left to die, so that in the dawn light the ashes could be searched for Brigit's Footprint.

The Churches of England and Rome roundly condemned such meaningless ritual. And the Secret Society of Freemasons had secretly abhorred the whole affair. But when the Candlemas Bride demanded a bridegroom it was a Chief Inspector who volunteered. He closed his eyes and thought of Scarman until the symbolic Brigit from Peterborough had done with him. And it was only when it was over and he reached for his trousers that he discovered he had no further use for them. He was bound, hand and foot, and instructed in the evils of patrilineal descent. And later, turkey-trussed and much wiser, he was finished off with a neatly severed windpipe.

There was a paralysed pause. No one seemed to know what to do next. It was not so much what had been done. The ungluing of marriages was common enough. It was rather the harsh finality of it. Even irrational marriages, based on physical attraction, could be ended without the shedding of blood. But the Molesworth sisters didn't give a toss. They had seen men at work. They had been on the wrong end of medicine and the law, and they were certain that they could draw on traditions just as ancient and idiotic. So, when a bridegroom had done what a bridegroom should do, they saw no healthy reason for keeping him. Brigit had ovulated. And if, in his last act, the Chief Inspector had failed to hit the bullseye, there would be other Brigits and other bridegrooms.

His men stood still, their perpetual fertility hanging like millstones round their necks. They could not move. Then came the blood bath. Forty men and horses perished that morning, and the ten wimmin who fell on their knives, rather than be taken, infected those left behind with a fever of sisterhood that would not be contained. And inevitably, with the wonders of modern travel and communication, East Anglia's problem of last year is Northamptonshire's of this.

Wimmin had taken to the streets in terrifying numbers. Wimmin of a certain age. Nearing forty they unleashed their bodies and sauntered in trousered gangs. Beyond sixty they stopped dying of breast cancer, and laughed too much. Most of them had husbands and had been kept for years in good homes with nothing more to do than push a damp rag around. Many of them had never been beaten. Even the ones that had asked for it.

And their families all asked the same bewildered questions. What more could we have done? Should we not have done so much? The effect on the children was heartbreaking to see. A few anxious daughters put aside their floor-polishers and tried to bridge the generation gap. A few sons got a grip and found their way to the kitchen. But the things that only a mother can do – the shortening of denim jeans, the replenishing of empty toilet rolls – these little jobs were left undone, and whole families went under. All that was left them was a deep sense of shame. It was not done to ask, 'And what's your mother doing nowadays?'

24

As Didge put on his bike clips, Swills passed him. He was carrying a wet bodywarmer.

'Good night, Mr Swills.'

'The modern toilet has got its limits.'

'Good night again.'

He wasn't alone in making a fast getaway. Most of the cars had gone already. Only Colin Cherish, delayed by a plumbing problem, was left to cross the car park on foot. And Kerry-Gene was waiting for him. Didge stood on his pedals for a better view as she goosed Cherish into dropping his keys, and then, as he gathered speed and rode by, Didge called out.

'Good night, Headmaster.'

Looking back over his shoulder he was in time to see Kerry-Gene liberating the shirt tail of authority.

There are those for whom work is a blessed release from the purgatory of family life. There are those for whom home is the sanctuary that makes working life tolerable. Not Didge. School. Home. They were all one to him. It was his nature to make the best of his circumstances and he had seen quite clearly that those who steer their own destiny with a cool sure hand are only faking it. Home in its shapeless shabbiness suited him. And Daddo and Hedley. Even the cat. The stuffing had shifted in all of them. Home had the agreeable lack of a woman's touch. They were comfortable together since Mother.

Mother had been a fine pleasant woman who ran her home well. She had married Daddo on the rebound and made it a happy partnership. She had cooked for him, borne him Filbert, and allowed him to take motor bikes to pieces on the front-room carpet, knowing perfectly well he would never be able to put them back together again. For his part he had done up inaccessible zips and once put a new flex on her iron. Didge remembered her fondly and laughed now at his childhood terrors. As a grown man he could smile at the thought of

25

Baking Day. But as a little lad he had hidden for hours to avoid the consequences of her batch bakes. And then there had been the jumpers she had knitted. It hadn't always been easy. But on the whole those had been happy days.

Then had come Hedley. Her legacy to them. He had been damaged, not by hurrying into the world too soon, but by coming reluctantly and late. Daddo had been sent for the nurse, but the British Legion Christmas Draw had to be decided that evening, and though eventually Daddo did return with a nurse and a canteen of cutlery, it was scant consolation for Hedley, whose brain had been expiring cell by cell.

Mother had marked time, until Hedley was of an age where she could form an impression, and around the time of his sixth birthday she came to the conclusion that he was a stupid, ugly boy who would be on her hands for ever. At that point she decided to die. It took several years but she was a determined woman. In time she went and, though Daddo seemed a little lonely, he struggled on. With her gone he had a great deal more room for his geranium cuttings, so it was, as he often observed, an ill wind.

At the Bingley turn Didge made a fatal error. He stopped to buy an evening paper and stayed a while, passing the time of day with Gerald behind the counter. When he emerged, the air was distinctly colder and, as he folded the paper under his arm, he was jostled by four wimmin. He hadn't seen them coming. They were just suddenly there.

He turned, trying to catch Gerald's eye, but Gerald had already seen and turned away, intent on topping up the Choc-Dip dispenser, leaving Didge alone with fear.

Then, where there had been four there were more of them. Eight, maybe ten. His mouth was too dry for counting. They pressed him heavily on either side and took his paper and his peppermints.

'Hello, sweetheart. Give us a smile.'

She couldn't have been a day under fifty. Didge's spirit flashed briefly.

'Give back my newspaper.'

'Give me a kiss and I might.'

'You've got a nice little bum. Hasn't he got a nice little bum?'

'A lovely little bum. Just crying out for it.'

'Stands to reason. All on his own. Loitering outside shops. When a man sits astride a bike like that it can only mean one thing.'

'Asking for it. Are they your own teeth?'

'He's trying not to smile.'

They ate his mints and leafed through his paper.

'Here you go: "Asthmatic Youth terrorised by Hags . . . I did not expect to survive, claims victim . . ."'

'"Fun-Loving Mothers. The Horror That Lurks at Home . . ."'

'"Bring back Agoraphobia and the Apron – a scarred generation lashes out . . ."'

'You shouldn't read this sort of thing, boy. It'll make you nervous. You'll end up too frightened to go out at night.'

'I'd like my paper back.'

'He'd like his paper back. You should get yourself home, darling. Get yourself home and put the safety chain on.'

'Shall we see you home? Shall we see him home?'

'We'll see you home. We wouldn't want a lovely little bum like that to fall into the wrong hands.'

'I think he's a bit of a tease. I've seen looks like that before.'

'Leaving it for some woman to make the first move. Play-acting passive. Come on. Pucker up.'

His back was pressed hard against the glass. Inside Gerald was double-checking the sell-by dates on the notepaper. Outside, men hurried by on the other side. Tall and grey, with her thumbs hooked over her trouser tops, she intruded wetly into his mouth, and he was aware that somewhere below another of them was toying with his arrangements.

27

When they'd finished with him, they tucked his newspaper into his saddlebag and moved away in a single body, loud, and taking up too much space. They discarded him with the wrappings of his peppermints. And still Gerald would not look up.

The shakes didn't start until he was nearly home. His bike carried him that far, and when he had to make it on his own from the shed to the door his legs wouldn't co-operate.

Should he mention it? Daddo might understand. He'd been a soldier. He'd seen life. And he'd lived all those years with Mother. Not that she would ever knowingly have done such an unhygienic thing. But it might have cropped up. Daddo might know of it.

On the other hand he might say things like 'Why didn't you scream?' and 'Wimmin never bother me'.

Better not to say anything. Better to get over it alone. And take precautions in the future. Practical steps. Be more watchful. Have the evening paper delivered. And wear an extra pair of underpants.

The stuff that headlines were made of had arrived in his own quiet life and nothing would ever be quite the same again.

Daddo and Hedley had a good fire burning and a quiz show to watch on the telly. Just like any other evening, there were pies to defrost and the sink to unblock. But events had moved Didge's orbit. He now saw different, more menacing horizons. He was spinning, gently and uncontrolled, through the maelstrom of Wimmin Power. There was a revolution on the way.

His only hope was that if he breathed in hard he might squeeze past it.

28

Chapter 4

Didge poured himself a stiff drink before he settled under the sunlamp. He had just spoken to Kit, and the line to Managua had been remarkably clear. Gemma and Nikki and Aspen came to sit with him for a while.

'Shall we talk to you, Didge?'

'That would be nice.'

'What shall we talk about, Didge?'

'I think we should go on some outings soon. Would you like that?'

'Outin's?'

'Trips. Excursions.'

'Going out?'

'Yes. To interesting places.'

'Where?'

'Well, where would you like to go?'

'Don't know really.'

'What would interest you?'

'Don't know really.'

'We could go to local places of interest. Like the Old Fire Station.'

'Dead boring.'

'Or the Magistrates' Court . . .'

'Been there.'

'Loads of times.'

'Or we could visit some local firms. Places where some of you might get jobs some day,' he fibbed.

'Can we go to the Cheddar Gorge?'

'Where?'

'Cheddar Gorge.'

'Why?'

'I don't know. It's supposed to be good.'

'Well we could bear it in mind for the spring. For the better weather. We don't have to limit ourselves to local things. We could go further afield. But just to start with we could try a few half days out. To places that are near.'

'And then we can bog off for the rest of the day?'

'No. No. Then you can come back to school and draw a picture of what you've been doing.'

'I know someone that could get us into the Dog Meat Factory.'

'Yes. Now that's the sort of thing, Nikki. Nikki's got the right sort of idea.'

'Banger.'

'What?'

'Banger. That's who she knows at the Dog Meat place.'

'No, it's not. I don't know Banger.'

'You done it with him once.'

'That don't mean he'd get us in. I know Razzer. We had the same Dad. He'd get us in.'

'I'm not going. I've smelt it.'

'That's only when it's cooking. It don't smell when it's cooled down.'

'We don't have it in our house. Bev says they use unfit dogs.'

'Razzer said that.'

'Do you have it, Didge? In your house?'

'What's that, Nikki?'

'Chunky Chuck.'

'Mm. We have lots of it.'

'Aaargh, Didge. It stinks. I'm not going. Do you know what they put in it?'

'I don't care. I love it.'

'They put poodles in it. And them little scrinny ones with the long hair.'

'Nonsense. The bone muscle ratio would be completely up the spout. Think about what you're saying, girl.'

'Well Boxers then. They put Boxers in it.'

'Do they? Yes, I suppose they probably do. They'd have to do something with them once they've been punched too much.'

'No. Boxers. Them dogs that show their bums all the time. They put all the gristly bits in. It all goes in.'

'Marvellous. Years ago, girls, when it was chicken and lamb, chicken and lamb, week in week out, I swore that if anyone ever came up with a scheme to rid the world of dog-shit, I'd give them every support. So I try to eat some every day.'

'Can we go to the biscuit factory?'

'What an excellent idea, Gemma.'

'Great!'

'I'll organise that. Excellent. And after Christmas perhaps we could even go to London.'

'What for?'

'What for? London is full of things to do. You could go to London every day of your life and still never see it all.'

'What for?'

'What for what?'

'What would you go to London for every day of your life?'

'To look at buildings. See pictures. Listen to plays. Hear music.'

'Get into fights?'

'I'd sooner go to the biscuit factory.'

'I think we could do both. The factory first. And further afield later. But you realise you won't be able to take that baby with you?'

'Haven't got him.'

'Why? What happened to it?'

'Gave him away.'

'Oh dear. Did they think it was for the best?'

31

'Who?'

'The Authorities.'

'No. I swapped him.'

'What for?'

'Leather trousers.'

'Leather trousers!'

'No, you never.'

'I did.'

'You haven't got no leather trousers.'

'I did have.'

'What have you done with them then?'

'Gave them to our Bev.'

'Why?'

'They didn't fit me.'

'No you never.'

A sudden noise brought Didge smartly into an upright position. Somewhere above them a siren was wailing. He looked helplessly from girl to girl and grabbed his shirt. He never knew how he tumbled into his trousers the right way round, and nameless panic prevented him from seeing that it was Aspen who did up his buttons. The alarm urged him on, into his jacket, into his shoes, and only after Mandy and Mia had both explained it to him did he even begin to understand.

Up in her crow's nest Dimity had spotted an intruder. The siren was only used when someone was approaching that might not be dealt with through the usual channels. Someone was coming that warranted a full alert. Rosalind.

Didge met her in the hall. She was calling up the stairs to Dimity.

'Stop that noise. You are a very, very, very wicked woman.'

He dipped his knees a little. Out of respect. And so that his trouser bottoms would fill the gaps where his socks should have been.

'Filbert! A matter of some urgency.'

'Rosalind! A rare but welcome visitor! Do come through.'

He opened the classroom door solicitously and checked his fly.

Those who weren't still hanging from the window calling up to Dimity were busy, cutting each other's hair and waxing their legs.

'And what are we doing this morning?'

'This morning, Miss Strutt, we are doing Health and Beauty.'

'What a wonderful idea.'

'Yes. Basically the theme is hair. Making the best of the stuff you want and getting rid of what you don't. As you can see, the girls are working round this central concept.'

'Marvellous. And I can see there are some very unusual hairstyles being created. Very unusual. And I hope Mr Didge has stressed to you the importance of keeping your brushes and combs scrupulously clean. My goodness, I wish I'd had opportunities like this when I was your age. I was still in pigtails when I was twenty. And when I went up to Oxford I found them very difficult to manage. I think it's a good idea to try new things. Strike out a little. I'd be interested to know what you think I should do with my hair.'

She sat in Didge's swivel chair and offered her head at various angles.

'Come along now, Mr Didge. I think you know all about these things.'

She didn't have a lot of hair. Didge was rather at a loss. He didn't want to touch it but he couldn't see how else she'd be satisfied. With the lightest of movements he plucked at the thin, colourless hair and Kandy came to his rescue.

'Grow it. She ought to grow it. And have highlights. And a perm.'

'Highlights? Would you say so? Well I might. I might.'

'There was something urgent?'

'I wouldn't want to frighten the horses . . . Yes, Filbert, there is something urgent. A staff meeting. An urgent staff meeting. At twelve. No time now for explanations. But do be there promptly.'

'We're going to the Cheddar Gorge.'

'Yes?'

'And the biscuit factory.'

'Well you're very lucky girls. Mr Didge seems to be going to a great deal of trouble for you. I hope you appreciate it. And, girls, it occurs to me we have a member of staff who might benefit from a little of your Health and Beauty. Some of you will have noticed how tired Mrs Corrigan is looking this term. I shall suggest she pops over to see you.'

Just before twelve Didge settled the girls with colouring books and sent Kerry-Gene to fetch his video cassette of 'The Living Planet', left behind on the draining-board in the rush to get out that morning.

'If it's my father, ask him to please check that it's the right tape in the right box. And, if it's my brother and he's there on his own, don't bother. And don't go into the house. It only encourages him.'

Chapter 5

It was the first time he'd been in the Staff Refuge that term. He'd never been fond of the place. Gathered in such numbers, the staff were vulnerable, and they knew it. It made for dismal, fragmented conversation, dogged by insecurity and fear.

Didge didn't care much for any of them. They favoured the kindly, intuitive approach to young people. Apart from Boyle. And Nutts. They favoured hitting people.

Didge felt the teaching profession had gone adrift somewhere. He had an idea that a little arbitrary cruelty might do children some good, but he didn't have a manifesto. Nothing he could put to Colin Cherish and say, 'Let's give this a whirl.'

He just felt there might be some middle road, as yet untried.

There was tension. Rosalind was right. Celia Corrigan did look strained. When he looked at her, volunteering to say something cheerful, she checked her hands for cleanliness. And then checked them again. Poor Celia. Trying to combine marriage and a career.

Everyone had said it couldn't be done. Fitting a quart into a pint pot. Skirting-boards left undusted. Husbands left to starve. The price was too high.

Didge knew Corrigan. He headed a special unit for boys who were technically inclined, a tebbity sort of chap who ran a tight and reasonable ship. Didge liked him and feared him. But he liked Celia, too. The girl was obviously spreading herself too thin. When had her net curtains last seen the inside of a washing machine? And when had Corrigan last had a hot meal? She was checking her hands again.

The door opened. Rosalind was first. She came to the seat next to him. It was something big. Cherish looked sombre. There was a stranger with him, dressed in the uniform of the School Inspectorate, and between them, sobbing piteously, was Tim Lull, Deputy Head of Liberal Studies and a wretched sight. He was uncuffed and allowed to sit with his greatest friend Amble. Boyle looked across at them scornfully. He despised the open-minded. He had made up his mind about everything in life so as to leave himself more time to reach peak physical form. Not like Amble and Lull. Types like that spent years making sure they'd seen things from everyone's point of view, receptive even at the eleventh hour to some paltry minority opinion. Wobblers. Wimps.

Amble steadied Lull with a reassuring arm and Headmaster began.

'Now, staff . . . we have had a serious complaint. Most serious. And I think Tim will go along with me . . . when I say that in the end it was a relief for him to get it off his chest. Regrettably, and I hope Mr Sniggs won't take this amiss . . . regrettably the Inspectorate has had to be involved. But there we are. I know we're all going to learn something from what's happened here today. And I know that Tim, who'll be leaving us for a while, leaving us so that he can have the time and space he needs to reflect on his behaviour and eventually, possibly, return to us full of sound resolve . . . I know that Tim will welcome a public airing of his mistakes because he recognises that we can all gain from his experiences. We can all learn. Yes. And that's the name of the game. We try it this way, we try it that way. Sometimes we think we can improve on the natural order of things, and sometimes, like Tim, we come a cropper. But we learn. And so, on behalf of the school, Tim, I'd like to wish you all the best for the future. It's been rather short

36

notice . . . but there will be a little something in the post for you next week. And you'll be most sadly missed. Most sadly . . .'

Cherish's voice grew husky. He lunged forward and shook Lull's hand. Amble urged Lull to his feet.

'Thank you, Colin, for those kind words . . .'

Sniggs disapproved of the informality and clicked the bones in his thumbs.

'. . . and for giving me a chance to make a clean breast. I know I'll go down at Freshfields as a rebel. Heroic renegade. Untamable insurgent. But I want to put the record straight . . .'

Didge leaned as near to Rosalind as was seemly and whispered.

'What's he done?'

'I've been thinking.'

'Yes?'

'You could take your girls to meet their Member of Parliament.'

'What?'

'Their Member of Parliament. You could take them to meet him. Help them to get the feel of things politically.'

Lull was well under way.

'Many's the hour Alan and Simon and Pam and I have prodded it around. And I have to say even now I'm not sure of the rights and wrongs of it. But if I've set discussions in motion, if I've got a few people questioning the bedrock of their attitudes, if I've reminded you all that we must constantly question and never be satisfied with what pass for answers, then it will have been worth . . .'

Rosalind hadn't finished.

'John Ryder Knight.'

'What?'

'John Ryder Knight. Our selected representative.'

'Yes?'

'I know him. I could arrange it.'

37

'I see.'

'He's terribly nice.'

'Yes?'

'I might even come with you.'

Lull had come to a stop. Tears, his own and other people's, had cut him short. Sniggs and Boyle looked at each other meaningfully and Amble helped his friend from the room for the last time.

'Rosalind.'

'Yes?'

'What has he done?'

'Heaps of things. He's very strong on constituency work. And since he's been a Minister he's banned heaps of things. Heaps.'

'Tim?'

'John.'

'John?'

'Ryder Knight.'

'No. What's Tim done?'

'Taught shredders to read.'

'Shredders? To read? My God. I'd no idea.'

'Three of his girls. They had firm promises of work at Central Shredding. He taught them to read.'

Didge whistled through his teeth. No wonder Sniggs had been called in. Central Shredding was the biggest employer in the whole Government Service. Recruiting standards were stringent but, once you were in, you were in. People had killed to reduce the competition. The work was repetitive and simple and the demand for it increased every year. Security and Shredding were the only cast-iron certainties left on the Career Officer's books. But it was vital that shredders should not be able to read. Everyone knew that. Everyone understood the good sense behind it.

'Bloody fool. He must have known he wouldn't get away with it.'

38

'He was reckless as to the consequences. And very short-sighted.'

'And what's done can't be undone.'

'Precisely. Three lives ruined. Three families disappointed. And for what?'

'I suppose they'll be able to read things. Books. And things.'

'That's what Tim said. In his statement. He wanted them to be able to read Great Books. But they won't.'

'Nobody ever does.'

'They'd have had security of tenure. And a pension.'

'Is Lull for the chop?'

'It's mandatory. Even if the Inspectorate hadn't been involved, Headmaster would have had no choice. He'd have had to have made an example of him.'

'What about Liberal Studies?'

'Alan and Pam will soldier on. I won't forget to contact John.'

'John?'

Everyone was dispersing. Headmaster was waiting for Rosalind to rescue him from Sniggs.

'Ryder Knight. I know he'll do everything he can to help.'

'Ah yes. Thank you.'

'Any time, Filbert. Anything to help.'

As he trudged back he wondered why Rosalind was being so decent to him. And Dimity. She let him through without hindrance. But inside there was bedlam. They had tired of the colouring books and were playing at Nobble the Outcast. Michelle was the heaviest and had been chosen to sit on Terri's chest. The others were seeing what they could push up her nose, but Terri was giving them no satisfaction. She had fallen asleep.

There was no sign of Kerry-Gene and the video cassette. All afternoon they talked about the biscuit factory and other ace places they might visit, and when Terri woke up she joined in and forgave them their beastliness. By the end of the day he almost liked them again.

Rosalind was waiting for him at her office window. The hairs on the back of his neck stood on end and the more he tried not to look in her direction the more he did. She mouthed 'I won't forget' and twiddled her fingers flirtatiously. And then she laughed. Didge pedalled away. Really fast.

They were toasting stale buns when he got home. He asked if Kerry-Gene had called but Daddo seemed not to hear. And Hedley wasn't reliable. Didge asked him more than once in words of one syllable but he just picked his nose with frantic thoroughness.

Daddo was restless. They ate the buns and had two pots of tea and all the while he fidgeted and suddenly remembered things. Didge wrote a letter to the biscuit factory and had to do it all over again because of the margarine stain. The moment it was sealed in its envelope Daddo pounced.

'Why don't you go out, son?'

'Out?'

'Post your letter.'

'It'll do in the morning.'

'You should get out more. At nights.'

'It's not safe out.'

'Course it's safe. Don't be so wet.'

'There's wimmin on the rampage everywhere. It's not even safe in the daylight any more.'

'Get away. No wimmin's ever kept me in at night.'

'Well you go out then. You never go out. And then you'll find out. They'll put the wind up you.'

'Balls.'

'That's one of the things they're after.'

'Knee them in the groin. That'll cool them off.'

'That's very nice. Have you ever kneed a woman in the groin?'

'Many's the time. It kept your mother tidy.'

40

'There's no pleasure in going out any more. Looking over your shoulder all the time. Avoiding the dark places. I'd rather stop in. If you go out and anything happens, people are just going to say what was he doing there, taking needless risks. Contributory negligence. That's what they call it. And it's not fair. It's not fair at all.'

'Nancy boy.'

That hurt Didge. Didn't he go out in all weathers to earn a living? Keep a roof over their heads? Didn't he look out for the pair of them? And go without? He had nothing to prove to either of them. Not a thing.

The zip on his anorak jammed, so he borrowed Hedley's and ran all the way to the post-box and back. But he was too late to impress Daddo. He had gone up to bed. It was eight o'clock.

Daddo came down again at ten to make himself a tray of supper. He never usually did such a thing, clipping his toe nails while the water boiled and humming, like he had at tea. And when he'd filled the pot he put a whole packet of lemon creams on the tray and cleared off upstairs, like a man without a care in the world. Didge shot Hed a suspicious glance. He laughed. And rubbed his knees together.

What was happening? Rosalind had been familiar with him. Daddo had hummed. And Hedley hadn't even whimpered when he'd looked at him sternly. Something was going on. Happiness was breaking out all over the place.

Chapter 6

'Are you hiding anything in your life? Anything at all?' He'd picked that up from The Richard Bumbry Hour of Prayer. Praise The Lord Logan held on to his hairpiece. He was welcoming Eighteen Plus Remedial to God's Goldenbake.

Didge had kept it all a secret until the very last minute. It had been a temptation to let the cat out of the bag on Friday afternoon when time was hanging heavy and Jacqui wouldn't stop banging her head against the window. But he'd been sensible. Hadn't let on to a soul even after the weekend. Playing along, doing dot-to-dot puzzles like it was any ordinary Monday.

Then, within twenty minutes of breaking the news, he'd walked them there. The stratagem had worked. The surprise had got as far as their legs, but was a long way short of their brains, and they had moved through the streets without incident.

Praise The Lord Logan was a big man anyway. And excitement had bulked him out. It was a long time since he'd received a party of visitors. So long that he'd had to come in on Saturday morning to search for the restraining harnesses. He'd been with Goldenbake for years, man and boy. He'd begun in the days when harnesses weren't necessary. Days when orderly groups of pleasant receptive youth had filed along the catwalks, peered into the vats and gone away again carrying a complimentary tin of shortbread and an informative pamphlet.

But times had changed here as everywhere else. A dull and sallow breed had been hatched. They threw foreign bodies into the uncooked dough and jumped on the complimentary tins. After several workers had been injured, legged over by resentful sightseers, the limb harness had been introduced. Ankle to ankle. Wrist to wrist. From that time on, those who still wanted to see the workings of a Christian factory were forced to shuffle in an educational chain-gang.

Didge explained about his eczema and was excused the harness but the girls were hooked together fast, before they had time to decide whether they minded.

Praise The Lord swelled above them. Even Didge looked small in the lee of those proud shoulders.

They were ready. Drums of golden syrup and factory walls bounded them on three sides. There was a fine undecided rain and a delicious smell of hot pastry.

'It is my duty to welcome you here today. A rare duty. I welcome you to God's Goldenbake and tell you that you will not see the like of this place anywhere else. We stand alone. Our workforce are healthy, in mind and in body. Our biscuits are peerless. And our workplace is a house of God. Those that labour in this godly place are without blemish. They pray for your salvation. Will you be saved?'

His great hands reached up towards the sky and the rain backed off.

'Will you be saved, sisters? The Lord is waiting for you. He truly loves those that come to him and repent. Will you be an instrument of the Lord? Will you do it today?'

Kandy was making unnatural suggestions to a man in a white boilersuit. Praise The Lord moved into top gear.

'As a jewel of gold in a swine's snout, so is a fair woman without discretion. I must ask you again. Are you hiding anything in your life? The Lord knows everything. There are no secrets from the Lord. Let us bow our heads in prayer. O Lord, inspire these miserable sinners in the hours ahead. Renew their faith, steady their resolve, and support their feebleness with your inestimable love. Amen. And the Lord

43

said, I will turn my hand upon thee and purely purge away thy dross and take away all thy tin.'

Didge looked up slightly. It seemed to be finished.

Logan had squared things with the Almighty and they were turning in through the double doors at the end of the block.

They saw it all. No effort was spared. They saw the weighing-room and the cold store. Ovens, hoppers, codes of practice, compulsory headwear, iced fancies, coconut whirls, hymn sheets, cherry thins, vanilla chubbies. They saw them all. And Didge nodded a lot.

The workers were all clean and silent, smiling at their nozzles and levers. There were no disputes, no frittering of time away from the factory floor conferring with brethren and undermining the profit ethic. At Goldenbake all aspirations and grievances were put before God.

They were about to go into the Chocolate Room. Someone was hissing Didge's name. Farah. She was paired with Tania at the end of the line.

'What is it?'

'We can't keep up.'

'It's rubbing.'

'What is?'

'The straps.'

'Nonsense. Just watch the girl in front of you and try to keep in step. It's only like marching.'

'It's rubbing. Look.'

Tania eased the leg of her jeans up with her harnessed hand and made Didge look at her ankle. The webbing had chafed the skin where it was thin over the bone and there was a small raw place.

'Hers is the same.'

'Have you looked?'

'She can feel it. I want to go home.'

Logan was about to lead the line off again.

'Slip them off. Quickly. Don't draw attention to yourselves.'

'They're too tight.'

'Your shoes, you stupid girls. Your shoes. Slip them off and step out of the harness. And stop whining.'

They helped each other to balance and freed themselves.

'Now get your shoes back on. And keep walking as though you were still attached.'

'What?'

'Shuffle, anaemia-brain. Pretend. Don't let on.'

And they went in. His mouth watered. He watched carefully as the ranks of freshly dipped chocolate fingers came over the crown of the conveyor belt and bore down on the chocolate finger checker sitting half way along. It was a job he wouldn't have minded himself. If it weren't for all that praying.

He could never say for sure when it was they had gone. Thinking it over later on, he thought he might have missed them in New Products when they had all been invited to try a Jimmy-Jammy. And yet he could have sworn they had been in the packing-room, and that was after New Products. The only thing that was beyond doubt was that, when the take-home tins of Raisin Rounds were being dished out, there were two too many.

After the first roll-call had been sabotaged he got really firm with them. He made them step forward in turn as he called their names and at the end his list told him what he had guessed anyway. Tania and Farah had gone.

Enquiries were made. They had been seen. Somewhere between the Jimmy-Jammies and the Chapel of Devotion they had done a bunk.

Praise The Lord Logan controlled himself. There was a lot he might have said but out of common charity he confined himself to the facts.

'They're gone.'

'Gone?'

'Gone to the ungodly.'

45

They had ducked out, back-tracked, legged it over a guard-rail, forced a door marked Strictly Private and gone. With a lorry driver.

'The ungodly?'

'They were seen to leave in a Plucol vehicle. Even as we speak, they are speeding towards the fleshpots.'

'Plucol?'

'Our sole suppliers of sodium pyrophosphate. Against Moab thus saith the Lord of Hosts, woe unto Nebo for it is spoiled . . .'

'Nebo?'

'Plucol.'

'I see. Couldn't someone have stopped them?'

'. . . Kiriathaim is confounded and taken. Misgab is confounded and dismayed . . .'

'Are they a local company?'

'London, sir. London. The trading estates of NW10.' Logan shook Didge's hand and pressed one of the spare biscuit tins on him.

'And the Lord go with you.'

'Didge! Didge!' Aspen was agitated.

'Is it something important?'

'Why has he gave us these?'

'What? Talk properly, girl.'

'Why has he gave us these biscuits?'

'Because this is a biscuit factory. And we have just visited it and behaved fairly well. It's a sort of gift.'

'But that's not what he said. Is it?'

'I don't know. What did he say, Aspen?'

'He said I will take away all thy tins.'

'It's all right. That wasn't quite what he meant.'

'That's what he said.'

'Yes. But it was out of the Bible.'

'Well, that's what he said.'

'Yes. But when people are saying prayers and suchlike they

46

don't usually say exactly what they mean. That's part of it. You have to wrap things up a bit. It's rather like talking to Headmaster.'

'We haven't got to give them back then?'

'No, Aspen. You can take them home with you.'

'But I don't want them. They're horrible.'

'I've never tried them.'

'Well you have mine then.'

And that was how Didge ended up with three tins of horrible Raisin Rounds.

Chapter 7

Tuesday morning there was a note for him. From Rosalind. It asked him to see her at his soonest convenience. She must have heard. Somehow the news had reached her that he had lost three girls and it was only December.

He was free until eleven. The girls had a double period of Attitudes with Dilly, so he ate two Cyprus Sherry Chocolate Novelties, straightened his tie and walked firmly across the divide between himself and the rest of the school.

Rosalind wasn't there. Her coat was on its hook and her outdoor shoes were standing on a square of absorbent kitchen paper. But no Rosalind. He hung around for a while, anxious to get the interview over and done with, and when she still didn't come he wandered down the corridor towards the class-rooms. He stopped by the notice board and looked at it. There was nothing on it. Staring into its greenness centred the mind wonderfully. He was beginning to feel euphoric and expanded, and then something brushed against his leg and startled him. It was Celia Corrigan, hugging the wall and hiding her face with her hands.

'Hello, Celia. Ready for Christmas?'

She peeped at him between her fingers.

'Christmas?'

'Ready for it? All systems go?'

'Too tired.'

'That's a pity. I rather like Christmas. People are nice.'

'Nice?'

'Parties. Parcels. That sort of thing.'

'Terence wants to see you.'

'Does he? How is he? I haven't seen him for a long time.'
'He wants to see you.'
'I'll come then. When shall I come?'
'He'll let you know.'
'Fine. We'll leave it like that then.'

Boyle and Nutts were approaching, on their way to target practice, biffing and bonking with their rolled towels. Didge wished Celia wouldn't huddle so. People would notice and make remarks if she carried on like that.

'I won't delay you then, Celia. I know this is a busy term for you.'

'Goodbye.'

'Celia . . . you didn't happen to see Rosalind up at your end?'

'A cripple. I saw a cripple trying to walk.'

'No, no. That wouldn't have been her.'

As Boyle and Nutts drew level she scuttled away.

'Hello, Celia.'

'Hello, Celia. Your hem's hanging down.'

Nutts came in close while Boyle sparred with the notice board.

'It's started then.'

'What's that?'

'It's started. We've heard.'

'Yes?'

'Corrigan wants to see you.'

'Yes. Celia said. I didn't know you knew Terence.'

'Corrigan wants to see you. Tonight.'

'Tonight. Yes, I should think that would be all right. Yes. It would suit me to pop over tonight.'

'Be there.'

'Certainly will.'

Boyle bobbed off and Nutts started to follow, running backwards. Then he came back, briefly, and in a gesture of solidarity fetched Didge one across his jaw.

49

The pain made him feel faint. He struggled to the Staff Stairs and sat down on the bottom step with his head between his knees, until the cold of the stone struck through the seat of his trousers. Somewhere, upstairs, a window shattered. He thought of signing off sick. Going home and having a condensed milk sandwich while the electric blanket warmed up. That way he could avoid Rosalind for another day. By tomorrow Tania and Farah would have found their way back, and Kerry-Gene and the missing video would have materialised, and everything would start to come right.

But he had left it too late. She had padded down the stairs so lightly that he had known nothing of it. She took his arm.

'Have you been hiding from me?'

'Rosalind!'

'Did you get my note?'

'I came looking for you. You weren't there. I saw Celia though. I was a bit concerned about her.'

'We all are, Filbert. The staff over here can talk of nothing else.'

'She should see someone.'

'Of course she should. But she's not an easy woman to persuade. And her husband has been less than co-operative. Between you and me I think he puts her under a lot of pressure. If you follow my meaning. But anyway I had a word with Wendy Wimble and Wendy had a heart to heart with her, woman to woman. And she got her to agree . . .'

People always gave in to Wendy after a short struggle. She went at them like a terrier and cheered them up until they went limp. Didge had a recurrent nightmare about having to play deck quoits with her. He wished the Dog Meat Factory would get her.

'So she's going to the Occupational Injuries Clinic on Friday and they're going to give her an iron injection. And Wendy's given her some Brewer's Yeast. To tide her over.'

'And that should do the trick, should it?'

50

'Brewer's Yeast? Never fails.'

'No. What I meant was, isn't it more serious than that? More than Brewer's Yeast can deal with?'

'I know what you're getting at. I did say to Headmaster that First Aid is all very well but it's no substitute for an expert opinion. So I'm glad she's going to the clinic. They see so many music teachers. I mean, they are recognised as being At Risk. And what I feel she needs is a massive supplement of vitamins A and D. Now what I wanted to ask you . . . was about Christmas.'

'Christmas?'

'Christmas. Will you be . . . around?'

'Oh, yes. We always are. And you?'

'Yes. Mummy and me. Why don't we combine forces?'

'Sorry?'

'Combine forces. For Boxing Day. Come for lunch. Stay for supper.'

'All of us?'

'Well, I wouldn't want to put your father and brother out at all. I expect they'd prefer to stay put. With it being such a family time of year. But they might spare you to come to us. Do you think?'

'What did you have in mind?'

'We usually have a roast. And a pudding with a touch of brandy. And then charades and hangman. We have enormous fun.'

'You see there's Daddo and Hedley to consider. I've never left them.'

'It's not that they wouldn't be welcome. It's just that Mummy's at an awkward age. With men. And I'd hate a scene. At Christmas. And then your brother would be very cooped up. We don't have a great deal of space. Or any special equipment.'

'No, nor do we.'

'What I meant was, at home I expect he knows all the places

51

where it's safe to fall. When he has a turn. We've got so many little tables, and bits of china. Nothing special, but I'd hate him to fall against something.'

'He doesn't have turns.'

'No, but they still need a lot of extra space, don't they?'

'Who?'

'People who are not quite right.'

'Perhaps I could think it over.'

'Oh, do think it over. I know you'll say yes.'

'I'll think it over.'

'I hope you didn't mind my asking.'

'No. No. It's very kind of you, Rosalind. Very kind. I'll think it over.'

She went her way as quietly as she'd arrived, but pinker. It seemed she hadn't heard about the girls. And, if it got to her now, her head might just be so full of festive thoughts that she'd be prepared to overlook it. He felt so relieved he didn't go home sick. He went back to the Annexe instead and made himself a toasted cheeseburger.

Chapter 8

All afternoon he played at not going to see Terence. He saw himself forced to cycle straight past the end of Long Furlong because of road blocks and marksmen and an escaped rogue Siberian Tiger. Or having to go straight home to bed with a raging toothache and a fat lip. Then he saw the Corrigans' house ripped apart by a gas explosion and its ruins flooded by a freak cloudburst. He even considered how it would be if Dimity pushed a whole sewing machine down onto him as he left the building, injuring him enough for hospital. Just for the one night.

He couldn't eat his tea. The fire was too hot and there was a smell coming from Daddo. Didge suspected that he had started wearing hair gel again. At seven he stood up to go.

'Going out, son?'

'Just for a bit.'

'Anywhere nice?'

'Only to see Celia and Terence. Professional colleagues.'

'Christmas party is it, son? Have you got to take a bottle?'

'No. Not a party. Just seeing friends.'

'Take a bottle anyway. I'll get you one.'

Daddo took a bottle from the cupboard where he laid his wine.

'There you are. Charmes-Chambertin '79. You can't say fairer than that.'

'I'm not taking wine. It's not a party. Celia's not well.'

'Take her a bottle of sherry then. Or port. Port's nice if you're feeling a bit humpty.'

'I'm not taking a bloody bottle. Not! Not! Not!'

'Stopping out long are you?'

'Shouldn't think so.'

'No need to hurry back on our account. And mind how you go.'

'All right.'

'Go steady on that bike then, son.'

'See you later.'

'Yes. Oh and, son . . . ? Would you say my hair was looking thick and bouncy?'

So he *was* using hair gel.

The Corrigans had a nice house on what was left of the Otters Brook Estate. A build-and-run merchant had put them up in the Seventies. Didge could remember the show houses being a favourite run out for people on a Sunday afternoon. But an undesirable element had moved in. They had come in droves with their patio sets and tried to do more than the fabric of the houses could stand. One couple in Barley Furrow had put in a minstrels' gallery, and when they got back from a fortnight in Ibiza the whole place had collapsed.

Didge rang the bell and someone looked at him through the peephole before unbolting the door. It was Boyle. Didge had made an outline of a plan. If it was Celia, he was going to be warm and reassuring, complimenting her on the colour of her jumper or the wonderful smell of home-baking. And if it was Terence he was going to go straight for it, man to man. A word or two about the weather and the Killerball Final on Saturday, and then to the nitty-gritty. Let him have it from the hip that friends could not stand by and watch Celia go to pieces.

But he didn't have a plan for Boyle.

Celia was on the stairs unable to come down. The way was blocked with packages from Titan Warehouses.

Terence came out from his sitting room. He looked well.

'Hello, Terence. How's tricks? Long time no see.'

'Were you followed?'

54

Didge looked at Celia but she couldn't help him.

'I see you've been buying up Titan Warehouses.'

Boyle explained, 'Fire damaged stock.'

'Is it? I've heard it's very hard to resist their bargains. Wardrobes are they?'

Celia smiled.

'Not wardrobes. A new nation. Terence is building a new nation. Aren't you, Terence?'

'That's it! That's enough! You've been warned. She's been warned. Answering back.'

Helped by Boyle, Terence hauled the Titan boxes out of his way and dragged Celia down by her wrist. She lost her footing, hitting every step on her way down, and then Terence twisted her arm up high on her back and hustled her through one door and then another. Boyle stacked the boxes back neatly and Didge wondered whether he should take his coat off.

'I came through the town. I can never decide if that's the quickest way . . .'

Terence came back alone and shut the door behind him.

'I was just saying . . . I can never decide which is the best way to come. I've got a feeling the Harborough Road is the quickest, but then it's uphill all the way home.'

'Were you followed?'

'Followed?'

'Check it.'

Boyle checked through the spyhole and gave Terence the thumbs-up. They went in. Not to the room with the piano that Didge had looked at from the street, but to a smaller room that was open to the kitchen.

'You've got it very nice in here now. Very nice. Is that what you'd call a breakfast bar?'

Nutts stepped forwards. He'd been standing by the fridge-freezer and Didge hadn't noticed him.

'Nutts! Hello again. I was just saying how nice this all is.'

Nutts showed him round. Inside the cupboards and the drawers and the waste-disposal unit. He demonstrated the pinger on the microwave, and the pepper-mill and the alligator's head padded oven-glove.

'It's all very nice. It really is.'

Terence sat down and then got up again. He thrust his hands deep into his trouser pockets and felt in them for the best way to start.

'I just wanted to say . . . well done, Didge. Well done. Good work. And are you with us all the way?'

Then he fell silent and left Didge to guess.

'We didn't know you were with us. We had no idea.'

Didge was glad he wasn't the only one.

'Brilliant cover. Absolutely brill. Nobody would ever think. You're the last man I'd have expected it from. So . . . well done.'

Didge was now wildly confused.

'It's very kind of you, Terence. How did you get to hear?'

'Intelligence.'

'Very bright of you.'

'We have our sources.'

'And how are . . . Things?'

'Marvellous, marvellous. I've just put a polystyrene cornice round the smallest bedroom, and all being well there's a new greenhouse being delivered next week.'

'And how are Things?'

'Oh . . . Things. Things are great. It's all go down at recruitment. Can't keep pace. I said to Pissy Hodge about the newsletters needing putting in envelopes and he said don't talk to me about pressure, I've got fifty to initiate over at Desborough and not a clean towel in the building. But we're getting there. We're getting the message across. All pulling in the same direction and that's what counts.'

Didge had now managed to understand that by pulling something in the same direction as Corrigan and Nutts he had achieved something praiseworthy. But what did Nutts pull in his spare time? That was the question.

'I shouldn't ask. I know I shouldn't. But we've been wondering. Are you with the Birmingham Cell? The word is you're with Edgbaston Covert Activities.'

He had been to Birmingham once. Cherish had sent him on a course, 'Climbing Frames – Which Way Now', after the Renaissance Garden had been done for. That had been in Birmingham. So he answered with imperfect truth.

'I have had connections with Birmingham.'

'That's what I thought. Covert Activities. Great! Your secret is safe with us. We'll all pledge secrecy with blood if you like. I'll get the knife . . .' ·

'No. Please don't. Your word is quite good enough.'

'I tell you what then, I'll put myself under Threat of Ordeal. How about that? I've been in for years of course. Joined after the Income Tax Riots. Felt the call. Knew I had to get in there and do my bit to stop the rot.'

'I'm not with anyone now.'

'No?'

'No.'

'Then come in with us. You've got to be with somebody.'

'Well . . .'

'No. Go on. Come in with us. We'd love to have you. Time's short and we want to be ready. For when He comes.'

'He's coming soon is he?'

'Who can say? I feel it though. Sometimes I feel He's very near. Come and be one of us. Be with us when He comes.'

'Of course I don't get a lot of time. What with marking and preparation. And Daddo doesn't like to be left.'

'But come when you can. One night a week would do. We have really good times. Blood vows. We do those. And educational talks. We have some lovely talks.'

'And exercises. They're the best.'

Nutts knew what he liked.

'Riding my old bike is about all the exercise I can manage these days.'

'No. Nutts doesn't mean exercises you do. Although we do. Because you can't build a healthy race on unsound bodies. No, he means exercises you go on. With tents. And billy cans.'

'And machine guns.'

'Didn't you have exercises in Birmingham?'

Didge's confidence was growing. He hadn't realised how simple it was to feel one's way around a strange and unlit conversation.

'No, we did other things. But I'm not at liberty to speak of them.'

They understood completely.

'But you come in with us. We're doing very well. Lull. He was a big one for us. Lull was a real triumph.'

'Lull?'

'You didn't know that was of our doing?'

'Rosalind said it was because of the girls. And the reading.'

Terence smiled.

'Rigged. My own idea actually. We guaranteed them a change of identity and relocation to Northern Shredding. Worked like a dream.'

'And can they read?'

'Not a word.'

'And Lull? His whole career sacrificed . . . ?'

'Right under Cherish's nose. He'll be the next. He's a doomed man.'

'I'm very out of touch with things. In the Annexe. It's easy to lose touch.'

'That's the beauty of it. Adds to your authenticity.'

'Do you think so?'

'Look at you. You're a shambles. Overweight. Suit fits where it touches. And you've got one of those soft, thoughtful-looking faces. I mean, now I know what I know, I can see you for what you are. The perfect cover job. Come in with us. You won't regret it. A man needs to belong. Think how you're going to feel when He comes and your membership's lapsed.'

'I'll certainly give it some thought.'

'And now have a drink with us before the night reclaims you.'

Nutts poured the boiling water into the cups of beef extract and Boyle carried them in very slowly. They were filled to the brim.

'And how do you see things developing?'

'Rapidly, Didge. Rapidly. That's how I see things. Keep a few breeders for their large womanly parts and shoot the rest. And you'll be doing your little bit. Three down and counting. Eh?'

He drew in some broth and considered things.

'I'm a ruthless man you see.'

'Yes?'

'Oh yes. I know what has to be done and I'm prepared to do it. For the general good. There has to be casualties.'

'I suppose that's what the general good has always been about. Casualties.'

'Of course it has. Weeding out. It's always gone on. You name me a civilisation that hasn't done a bit of weeding out. You can't.'

And he couldn't. Not without prior warning and a few reference books. He tried his drink again but it was still too hot.

'And after the weeding out? How do you see things going after that?'

'Tidying up. There'll be years of it. Mopping up little pockets. I shan't get any rest in my lifetime. I'm quite resigned to that. There'll always be work to be done. Always some new pestilence being got up by the enemies of society. Spongers. Pacifists. Integraters. It never ends. Nests of them hidden under things. Organising. Fermenting. Fomenting. Studying things. But we've got to get to grips with the wimmin first.

59

That's the priority. That's what I'm getting on with. When He comes He might want to go for something else. Till then I'm getting on with it. For the general good.'

'And general happiness?'

'Happiness?'

'General happiness.'

'Safer to do without it I'd have said.'

'Terence, I wouldn't want to pry . . .'

'No. I wouldn't want you to.'

'But I did wonder about Celia.'

She must have heard her name. Her face appeared, pale and odd against the glass of the kitchen door, making Didge jump and scald his chin. She was shut out in the garden with only a cardigan for warmth. Her voice was faint through the door.

'I think I'll come in now, Terence.'

'She is an old friend, Terence. And she does seem to be in difficulties.'

'That's natural. You'll have seen her at school. It's natural you should wonder.'

'We've all been worried. Actually she seems to be outside the kitchen door. She's trying to attract your attention.'

'Attention's exactly what it's all about, Didge. But she responds very quickly to the medication.'

'Do you think she needs a holiday?'

'You never married did you, Didge?'

'No.'

'No. Well there you are.'

'It's just that she seems to be locked out without a coat.'

'It's a woman's problem. Phantom menopause. It's all in her mind. She's had all her insides out so we wouldn't have any trouble with it when the time came, so she's doing it all in her mind instead. She knows what she's doing. It's all a bid for attention.'

'A phantom menopause?'

'Yes. They're getting very popular.'

60

'I'd no idea.'

'No, well . . . as I said. When you've never been with a woman like I've been with Celia.'

'I certainly didn't mean to interfere.'

'I know that, Didge. Forget it. Consider the matter closed.'

'I must go.'

'Yes you must.'

Didge left his drink. Nutts and Terence both gripped his arm in a mysterious farewell and pledged themselves right there by the breakfast bar.

'ManPower.'

'ManPower.'

And, as Didge didn't have anything on for the next few seconds, he said it as well.

'ManPower.'

Boyle checked for undesirables outside the front door and then Terence urged him to be gone while it was safe. 'Be careful, Didge. We are all targets. And come and join us soon.'

'Thank you for the drink.'

'You were never here.'

'What?'

'Never heard of you. Word to the wise. Know what I mean?'

And, although he didn't, Didge said that he did and unlocked his bike. He did wonder about sneaking a pullover round the back to Celia but he decided against it. It was best not to interfere in medical matters. Warmth might aggravate it. He couldn't recall Mother ever having anything like it, but she'd never had attention anyway so she might not have known about it. He resolved to look it all up in the United Dairies Encyclopaedia of Diseases and then he biked home fast along the well-lit route before any wimmin got wind of him.

His key turned in the lock and the door gave a little, but it wouldn't open. There was something heavy the other side of it, and a lot of activity . . . The kitchen light went on and then off.

Daddo's voice was raised. The cat squealed. And then the hall light came on and the door suddenly gave way under his weight. It was Hedley. Letting him in and looking normal.

He went over the place thoroughly. The table was exactly as he had left it. The breakfast dishes were still in the sink. The television was hot, the paper was tucked down the side of Daddo's chair, and the length of tinsel that had come adrift by the window was still swaying in the breeze.

'What's been going on?'

'On?'

'What's been going on? I couldn't get in.'

'Lock's probably froze.'

'Not the lock. There was something against the door.'

'That was the draught-stopper. You must have trapped it when you pushed.'

'Rubbish.'

'It might have been Hed. He was just checking the draught-stopper. I'd just said to him there was a terrible draught.'

'Well something's going on. What about the cat? Why did the cat squeal?'

'Oh, yes. I can explain that, son. I kicked it. It was thinking of doing its business over in that corner.'

'That cat never does its business in that corner.'

'Well it was thinking of it.'

'I shall get to the bottom of it you know. I'm not stupid.'

'You weren't out long, son. Have a nice time?'

'It was just business. Just business.'

Didge wasn't sure of his ground. It was possible that they'd been wrapping his Christmas present. In which case it would be ungracious of him to press the issue. But he had a feeling that someone wasn't telling the truth, and when he looked the cat in the eyes she looked back steadily and dared him to say it was her.

Chapter 9

Under two niggardly duvets and a layer of pink candlewick, Didge stretched, yawned, and sniffed his fingers rapturously. It was ten o'clock and there was no need to move. He watched the wallpaper until he got the pattern of double-headed elephants and thought about sausages, hot tea and the purpose of life.

Eight days until Christmas. The little matter of a gift for Rosalind could not be put off for much longer. She was sure to have something for him. As soon as he'd said 'Yes' she'd gushed with plans, and he knew from the festive issue of *Woman's Friend* that lay well-thumbed on her desk, that she wanted everything to be perfect. He had held out for a while. He didn't want to offend her, but he did like Christmas the way he did it. Trimming up, letting everyone have the TV dinner of his choice, arguing over the *Guinness Book of Records*. He'd been on the point of saying he wouldn't. And then Daddo had let it out. Bent over, inspecting his verruca, he'd let it drop that he'd invited Twice Nightly Tufnell for Boxing Day. Suddenly a day with Rosalind and her mother had its attractions.

He'd brought it on himself, really. Mother had never held with visitors, and since she'd gone he'd encouraged both of them to have their friends in. To treat the place like home. He had hoped that an open-door policy would lead to a circle consequential enough for a fork supper, but it had never got off the ground. A girl had called once to ask after Hedley. He'd exposed himself to her several days in a row and then he'd caught a chill and missed an evening. She'd called to check on

63

him. And Daddo had his allotment friends. But Didge had never been able to break their years of conditioning under Mother. They would never come further than the back step because of the mud.

So for Daddo to suddenly invite Tufnell. And for Boxing Day . . .

Didge was wholly against the idea. Christmas was a time for family. Tufnell wasn't family. It was hard enough to welcome him in the middle of August. Unsavoury things were said of him. His name had been linked with unnatural practices at the Evergreen Drop-In Centre, and he had once invited Didge to bulk buy his personal requisites at a substantial discount. He couldn't understand what Daddo saw in the man. They were both widowers, but they had travelled very different paths to that shared condition. Mother had been in charge of her own passing. Mrs Tufnell had gone before she was ready, flat on her back with a safety-pin holding one of her shoulder straps.

But Daddo wouldn't be budged. He was prepared to attest that Tufnell would be full of fun and surprises, and, as if that were not testimony enough, that the man would bring his own booze with him.

So Didge said 'Yes' to Rosalind and landed himself a problem. What did one buy for the woman that had everything? The only thing was to catch a bus to Northampton and see what there was.

He dressed quickly to keep the cold out and rubbed his shaver round his chin. Daddo was out. There were no sausages and Hedley was at the table, engrossed in his mail order catalogues, with the light still on.

Hedley spent too much time looking at pantyhose. Didge wouldn't have minded if he'd looked at men's things sometimes. Torque wrenches, loft ladders, that sort of thing. But it was always women's wear.

64

It occurred to him that he could take Hedley with him. Should take Hedley with him. But he'd have to find his shoes and his bus-pass, and as soon as they were on the bus he'd want the toilet. It was easier to leave him.

There had been a heavy frost, so Didge went cautiously. He bent his knees like he'd seen on 'Let's Go Ski-ing'. Coming towards him, wider than anyone needed to be, with a litre of One-Cal Cola under her arm, was Glenda. She wasn't bending her knees. She had no call to. She had her Ice Grippers strapped round her slippers and her step was confident.

'You on holiday again?'

'Yes. Christmas holidays.'

'You ought to get a proper job. I feel sorry for your Dad.'

Glenda's opinion of teachers was unspeakably low. Life had treated her shabbily but she could at least comfort herself that none of her lads had sunk that far. She had groomed her three sons for proper manhood. She'd gone without so they could have shooting lessons and boxing lessons. Her dinette had been lined with books on racial purity and physical excellence. Glenda had done everything a mother could do, but in the end, despite the steaks and eggs and moral guidance, their minds had walked out on her. Brett had become a nurse. Carl and his friend had their own pottery in the Cotswolds. And Gregg had broken his mother's heart. He had promised he would have stamina and muscle, but he'd overdone the anabolic steroids with the lager, and one summer morning pharmacology had played a trick and he had woken up as black as the ace of spades. So she'd had her disappointments. But it seemed to her that Daddo's had been greater, and that helped.

'Ready for Christmas, Glenda?'

'Stuff Christmas. How's your Dad's back?'

'All right I think. Has there been something wrong with it?'

'It's easy to do your back in at his age. When you're overdoing things.'

65

'He's very well. Taking life at a steady pace. He keeps very well.'

'Got your turkey?'

'No. It's not worth it for three. You must find that. Being on your own. There's too much on a turkey.'

'I've got a twenty-four pounder indoors. I couldn't get a bigger one.'

'Any of the boys coming?'

'I love turkey. I could eat it and eat it. I hear Tufnell's coming.'

'Yes. I shall be spending the day with friends so it'll be company for Daddo and Hed.'

'I shouldn't like to think I was leaving an old man and a mental defective with Tufnell. I wouldn't want that on my conscience.'

She kicked her gate open and went in.

There were things to collect at the Post Centre. A seed catalogue for Daddo, an insurance reminder, a letter from Susan and Douglas in the land of milk and honey, and a Christmas card, a robin in a party hat, from Clem and Arthur. He wondered about that. He thought Arthur was dead.

Outside the Post Centre he made a decision. A new pair of trousers. For Boxing Day. And to ensure that he'd be looking his very best in a thirty-eight inch waist he detoured round to the school to see how things were and collect the Vibraslim belt.

The metal detector at Main Gate was under its plastic cover, and in the car park only Swills' electric three-wheeler and the usual police van were parked nose to nose, their windscreens sprayed with seasonal Glitter-Sno.

There was a smell in the Annexe. Someone had left something and it had gone off. He grabbed the Vibraslim, put it in his bag and locked up again.

People were moving about in Headmaster's office. In case Rosalind was in there making a list he decided to skirt the whole

66

of Main School and leave the back way. As he left the protection of the Annexe doorway a window opened above him and he was struck on the hip by a can of condensed cream of tomato soup. When Dimity had his attention she called down, 'Merry Christmas!' and shut the window firmly before he could reply.

Swills came out of the Humanities Fire Exit so swiftly there was no avoiding him. His shoes were dark with stickiness. He'd been busy with his sponge and bucket.

'Hello, Swills. Ready for Christmas?'

'They'll have to fill in a G46. I've got no authority.'

'There's a nasty smell in the Annexe if you've got a minute.'

'I shouldn't even have done this. It's my day for windows. I told him. Get your P13 done in triplicate and bring me the bottom docket. Then we'll see.'

'Perhaps you could track it down tomorrow? If you're pushed for time now?'

'Tomorrow?'

'The smell.'

'Smell?'

'In the Annexe. There's a bad smell.'

'I know. She used to teach needlework.'

'I'll leave it with you then?'

'It's not my week for smells.'

Swills tipped a bucket of redness down an outside drain and Didge hurried for the twelve o'clock bus. If it was running. Since Operation Island in the Sun there was no one left who knew or cared how the public were to get about the country. If the twelve o'clock didn't come there was no telling. He could wait for hours.

The Supa Center was crowded. Every window was dark, boarded against looters. Only the laser lights lifted the mood of the place.

He had just found some trousers in Brummels when he

67

spotted them. Michelle was picking up jumpers two at a time and putting them back one at a time. She passed one of each pair back to Kandy, who let it fall to the floor to be scooped up by a third party and hidden under the raincover of a pushchair. The child tucked up with the jumpers had familiar features, and although he never saw more than the back of its mother's head, he knew anyway that it was Fleur. She had thickened a little since she'd been expelled but Didge knew her back view better than he knew her face.

He had the trousers wrapped without verifying the size and hurried on before Fleur noticed him.

He had decided on something perfumed for Rosalind. In Magnadrug he had to fight his way through some ugly scenes. There was panic-buying in Prosthetics. He'd never seen anything like it. There had been something on the news the night before. Something about shortages. People were piling their trolleys with dentures and artificial limbs as though the place were closing down for ever. The pacemaker shelf was completely cleaned out and real teeth and hair were flying as two men wrestled on the floor over the last silica breast implant. Didge was appalled. He picked up a six-pack of glass eyes, just in case, and moved on to the Fragrance Department.

He chose soap for Rosalind. And then, in case that looked too mean, he went back for the dusting powder, and a box of perfumed drawer liners for Mrs Strutt.

He felt well satisfied with his afternoon. He had a Four Seasons Pizza, two cups of coffee and a slice of fudge cake, witnessed two grievous assaults and watched a show of strength by the uniformed wing of the British Bulldogs. When he came out into the real world the stars were out and there were no buses running.

He had walked for nearly two hours when he saw the lights of Moulton. He regretted the weight of the Vibraslim and the hole in his right sock. His feet were tender, the memory of the fudge cake had faded and he was very near to tears. He leaned

68

for a moment against a street lamp and eased his blistered toe inside his shoe.

A car slowed alongside him and a pleasant-looking woman wound down her window.

'Kettering?'

'Yes.'

'Hop in.'

'Are you going all the way?'

'Can do.'

She leaned back and opened the rear door from the inside. Fulsome with gratitude Didge climbed in, turning his back on Northampton and all that his mother had ever told him about getting into strange cars.

Moving at fifty miles an hour along a deserted road in the company of four unknown women he was right to feel uneasy. He never really saw their faces. The one next to him ran her arm round him, feeling for the opening of his coat. The one in the front passenger seat tugged his pullover free of his trouser waistband and pried at the place where he had asked too much of the fastener and it hung loose. From beginning to end she was the only one that spoke.

'Dressed a bit . . . provocatively, aren't you?'

Chapter 10

They cremated Celia the day before Christmas Eve.

Didge heard after it was over. Glenda knew someone who had a daughter who knew someone. She said Swills had found her in the music-room, that there had been enormous amounts of blood and that she had had a smile on her face. She'd tidied up before she did it, cleared her drawers, stitched up her skirt hem, and defrosted the fridge. But she'd left no letter. No clues. No apologies. No consideration. Luckily the floor was washable and there was some paint in Swills' cart that was a decent match, so he was able to have everything as it should be before he locked up for the holiday.

Didge kept going over it. Even when he was unwrapping his thermal vests and being pleased about them, it was in his mind that Celia was through with Christmases. It made him gloomy. He went out for a walk before tea at Daddo's suggestion. The lamps were coming on. Doors were shut against the mist, and behind them tins of salmon were being opened by people with murder in their hearts. He walked and walked and saw no one. He gave no thought to his safety, despite a faint bruised reminder of what can happen to a man who runs risks, for he was absorbed by certain facts. Celia had been. And now she was not. And that was all.

Didge wasn't due at Rosalind's until twelve but he had to get out of the house. Tufnell had arrived before breakfast with two bottles of vodka and a laundry bag full of Viewmaster Disciplinary Delights, and set about irritating him.

The sniggering made him drip juice from the can of sprouts

he was opening for their dinner, and he was secretly glad that he'd have to change back into his old faithfuls. His new trousers were tight everywhere. He hadn't had the heart for the Vibraslim after Celia. And the lighting was odd in Brummels. He'd bought them for grey and now they were lilac. Tufnell was being pointed.

'You courting yet, Filbert?'

'No.'

'Only I'd heard it was your lady love you was trysting with today.'

'No.'

'I mean, Boxing Day.. It's not a day as you'd spend away from your family without good reason. Not a family man like you. Not unless it was a very tasty little bit of skirt.'

Hedley was scraping the custard pan. He'd be at it till tea time.

'I'm just lunching with friends.'

'Nice is she?'

'She's a friend.'

'Nice legs?'

'Legs?'

'Nice are they?'

'They're just legs.'

That wasn't quite true.

'I like legs. Your mother had very nice legs. Lovely. Glenda. Now she's got very ugly legs. Terrible. Very bad veins. Has your little lady got veins at all?'

'I've never looked.'

Daddo and Tufnell heard that and watched the Dancing Magicoals in silent disbelief. Then Daddo forgot what he had forgotten every day since the North Sea Gas had been piped in and cleared his chest onto the back of the fire. It sizzled there, changing its shape, and Tufnell tried a different tack.

'Are you a bum-bandit then?'

'Sorry?'

71

'No need. There's a lot of it about. I'm as broadminded as the next man.'

'Yes?'

'Oh yes. What you do behind closed doors is your own sad affair.'

He went to Long Furlong with a note of sympathy for Terence but the house was closed up. A woman opposite lifted her nets and shook her fist at him but he didn't stop to ask her what she knew. He went to the Parks instead and sat for a while on a wet bench looking at the duck tableau. The only ones that still had heads on were the ones at the back that were difficult to reach. A school party had passed that way.

There were sniffers everywhere. There were ones that were still moving, on the swings, passing the sniffy and being neighbourly. But many of them were still enough to be dead, and some were too still for him to dare to look at. On the next bench one of the dead men pulled his coat closer round him. Didge checked again that he had the Strutts' parcels in his bag and left the way he had come.

Rosalind was wearing lipstick.

'Presents! Filbert! How lovely! I've got something for you, of course. Just a little something. Are you well? Oh, isn't this fun! Mummy's in the morning-room. I'm glad you got here early. Now I can brief you on who's coming.'

She took the parcels and his coat and bag. It was a very cold house.

'Tom and Nesta Galloway are coming for drinks if they're back in time. And Babs and Guy Hinchcliffe. And Canna and Stroma. The Chisholm sisters. But you'll know them. They're all heavily booked but they said they'd move heaven and earth to get here. And best of all, a bit of a coup, though I say so myself, John said he'd pop in for a quick one.'

'John?'

'Ryder Knight. I knew you'd be glad of the chance to meet him socially. Before you take the girls to meet him. Of course he's frantically busy, so we're jolly lucky.'

Didge was pleased he hadn't worn the lilac trousers. 'We'll have a little drink while we wait for the others. Come in and meet Mummy. She's having one of her good days.'

This was not a moment Didge had looked forward to.

He had known Rosalind for a long time but he had never met her mother. Her reputation was considerable. Rosalind talked of little else. Mrs Strutt rarely left the house except to go to Northern Italy where the air suited her. She kept the telephone locked, disapproved of pleasure, and had completely sabotaged Rosalind's emotional development by following her to Oxford and taking a suite at the Randolph for three years. She had been a burden and a trial to Rosalind who had borne it as dutifully and well as might be expected of an only daughter.

Mrs Strutt was sitting close to an electric fire. It had one sulky bar just showing pink. The first thing he noticed was that she only had one head. Then he noticed that it was beautiful. She had a lot of hair, piled like an auburn meringue, and everything else, from her earrings down to her leather boots, was unapologetically purple. She swivelled in her chair as Rosalind spoke her name, paused to recall why there was a strange man in her house, and then, with an unscrupulously easy smile, knocked Didge for six. She was a cracker. A geriatric cracker.

'You must be Filbert. Sit here and let me look at you.'

She lit a small cigar and settled back to inspect him.

'And did you put up much of a struggle?'

'Sorry?'

'I was just wondering what Ros had done to persuade you to spend a whole day in this terrible house.'

'Yes?'

He let her have a tentative smile and she repaid him immediately.

'Can it possibly be that home is worse than this?'

'It was very kind of her to invite me. And kind of you as well. With not knowing me.'

'Nothing to do with me, my dear. Not that I mind. I like people. I like to have them around. Making noise. Dropping things on the rugs. Ros tells me you have a father and a brother. Do pour some drinks, dear heart, Filbert looks perished.'

He couldn't find the right voice. He wanted to match hers for resonance, but it wouldn't come. He had to make do with his usual one. Rosalind poured them each a Slimline Tonic.

'Yes. There's just the three of us.'

'And Ros didn't invite them because your brother is special.'

'Handicapped. Yes. Well not even that really. He's a bit slow. Finds it hard to fit in.'

'And does this special brother have a name?'

'Hedley. We call him Hed.'

'Well here's good health to Hed and to anyone else that can't fit in.'

So the two of them raised their glasses. It was Didge's first drink of the season.

'And tell me about your father.'

'He keeps very well. Considering. He's very fond of gardening. Likes to be out in the fresh air.'

And here he fibbed, because lately Daddo spent most of his time locked in his bedroom having nightmares.

'Does he! I hate it. We have lots of garden here. Far too much. I should like to get rid of it all. Ros first, then the kitchen, then the garden, I'd get rid of them all. Darling, is there anything in these drinks we should get excited about?'

Rosalind was at the window watching the road. Mrs Strutt undid her parcel and sniffed at it.

'How very lovely. And how clever to choose something when we'd never met. I don't think I could have been so clever. Now. We've established that you have a wise brother and a misguided father. So next you must tell me about yourself . . .'

74

'Nothing to tell really. School keeps me pretty busy. I don't do a lot else. I know I should. Daddo's always saying I should join a club or something.'

'Oh no, Filbert. Don't do that. It wouldn't be a good idea at all. I'm a lot older than you and one of the things I've learned is that joining things is nearly always a bad move. And you have charge of the Big Girls at school?'

'Yes. The Easter Leavers.'

'Aren't they dismal? I think you're terribly brave. People despise teachers without stopping to consider what's involved. At least it's girls, though. In principle, I'm in favour of girls. Aren't you, Filbert? They can have an improving effect in most situations.'

The telephone rang in another room and Rosalind went to attend to it. As the door closed Mrs Strutt leaned towards him and took his glass. From under her embroidered jacket she pulled a long thin plastic bag filled with colourless liquid. It was a colostomy bag.

'Darling boy, let's give your drink a little help.'

He hesitated long enough for her to understand.

'It's all right. It's only gin. If Ros smells it, I'll own up. Tell me, how's Dimity these days?'

'She's up above me. Do you know her then?'

'Used to. Marvellous old dear. Well, she's younger than me of course. Dear Dimity. She had a bit of spirit.'

'They don't bother about her now. They closed the needle-work department.'

'Quite right. Needlework should never have been taught. It diminishes the mind. I don't know how Dimity managed. It never diminished her. I think it distilled something in her instead. Anger probably. Yes. And what about Celia?'

'I didn't know you knew her.'

'Hardly at all. They came here from time to time. She probably did the right thing. She was too feeble to get the better of a man like Corrigan. I've known him for years. He

75

was a chorister when Selwyn was at Peterborough. No . . . it was a struggle to the death I'd say. She could have loosed the stair-rods and invited fate to take a hand. I would have. But that's the trouble with religion. It stops you organising things.'

'Did you go to the funeral?'

'No, no. Ros went. I always vomit in churches. Ros's father was a bishop, you know. Have one of these little soggy jobs.'

She passed him a plate of canapés and topped up his glass just in time. Rosalind returned looking glum.

'That was the Hinchcliffes. They're stuck at Spalding with the Rodwells.'

'Poor Rodwells! What are your family doing today, Filbert?'

'They've got people in for lunch. Only a small party.'

'Ros has invited a dreary bunch. I think she's going to make you play Musical Chairs with the Chisholm sisters so this will be a Christmas you'll never forget.'

By a quarter to one Rosalind was plucking threads from the curtains like a woman possessed. Mrs Strutt and Didge, both the worse for the gin that they'd sneaked every time Rosalind thought she heard the telephone, were cosy round the electric fire comparing notes on the sights of Padua and Siena. A car stopped outside.

'Is that the Chisholms?'

'It's your taxi.'

'Is it that time already? Help me up!'

She leaned on her stick while she told him that he was to call her Bella and was to come back and see her very soon.

'I have enjoyed meeting you, Filbert. I shan't see you again today because I intend to stay out very late indeed, so I'll wish you all the best with Ros's lunch.'

Chapter 11

As soon as she'd gone, Rosalind rearranged the biscuits round the tuna dip and turned off the fire.

'Sorry about Mummy.'

'She's very nice.'

'I hope she didn't embarrass you. Anyway she's gone. So now it's just us.'

They toyed with their empty glasses and re-ran the story of Celia and the kitchen knife until the smell of cooking couldn't be denied and Rosalind seemed ready to admit that no one else was going to show up.

'I expect John's been called back to London. Urgent government business.'

'He'd be on holiday wouldn't he? They won't be sitting on Boxing Day.'

'There might be a crisis. We wouldn't know. He might be in a Think Tank. He's a public figure you see. He never knows what the next telephone call may bring. And Tom and Nesta are having a downstairs extension. So there's no telling.'

'I suppose you'll have cooked too much?' Didge was hopeful.

'I'll freeze some of it. I hate waste.'

The dining-room was colder than the morning-room. He sat there alone, while Rosalind came to an agreement with the beast in the oven. He called through a couple of times to see if he could help, but she was a woman who preferred to face failure alone. Straight off he could see it wasn't a turkey. It wasn't even a steam-roasted starling. It had neither wings nor legs so it was impossible to guess how it had gone about its business or how it had met its end. But Rosalind had got it to submit and she had piped it with rosettes of mashed potato.

'Smells good.'

'I hope it's all right. I gave it a bit longer than the book said. I don't care for lamb when it's underdone.'

'Lamb! Mmm! I don't think I recognise the cut. It looks very interesting.'

'Rolled breast. Stuffed with egg, breadcrumbs and sardines. Will you carve?'

He cut through a good deal of string and fat and eventually reduced the thing to smaller pieces. Rosalind said she could only manage two tiny slices, so he felt it would be bad form to take more than three for himself. And although he was ravenous he finished long after her, on account of the sardines.

'I hadn't realised your mother would be going out. I didn't think she got out very much.'

'She goes out to be awkward. She can be a very difficult woman. If she doesn't like the people that are coming.'

'You should have said. You could have come to my house instead.'

'No. I didn't mean you, Filbert. It was probably the Hinchcliffes. Or Canna. She says Canna never listens. Shall we pull our crackers?'

They made hilarious noises and put their paper hats on. Didge called out the mottoes while she was in the kitchen putting the kettle on for the custard.

'Where do policemen live?'

'No. I give up.'

'Letsby Avenue!'

She laughed too much.

'What's black and comes out of the ground shouting Knickers Knickers? Rosalind? What's black and comes out . . .'

'I wouldn't know.'

'Crude oil!'

78

It was his turn to overdo the laughter. The pudding was so small he forgave Mrs Strutt for abandoning him.

'Where was your mother going?'

'To the Imperial. There's a crowd of them. Old girls.'

'That's nice.'

'I find it pays. The Imperial's very pleasant. And she doesn't get so restless if I let her do something like that.'

'I wonder if Daddo would like it.'

'What I like is you don't get the more . . . disruptive elements. Well I say that but we did have a nasty incident with Mrs Finch. Mummy was quite friendly with her, although she was a Methodist or something. And then she went off in one of those gangs. Stopping men in the street. Touching their bodies. I kept Mummy in until it had blown over. I mean with Daddy having been what he was I have a responsibility. Not that Mummy could have gone off because she's got a silly hip. But that woman might have taken advantage of her. She'd only to have asked and Mummy would have taken in letters and cashed cheques. She can be very naive. I know I shouldn't complain. She's good for her age. Really. Now it's time for you to open your present.'

She fetched the parcel from the sideboard and Didge undid it elaborately.

'Handkerchieves!'

'I thought they'd be useful.'

They were white cotton. With embroidered initials. The letter S.

'And initialled . . .'

'No one will notice. And they're such good handkerchieves. Daddy would have hated them to have gone to waste.'

'Well I shall certainly use them. Thank you very much, Rosalind.'

'It's difficult to know what to give a man who has so much.'

They sat over their cups of coffee-flavoured Cuppadrink. There was no sign of the stilton or the port.

'Is there any chance that Mrs Strutt will be back?'

'Why? Are you planning to overpower me while I'm defenceless?'

'I just wondered.'

'Mummy won't be back for hours, so we can really relax. I thought we'd have a truly traditional afternoon.'

Didge rallied at the prospect. The fire would be turned back on. All three bars. He would select a cigar. And an after-dinner sticky. And then Mrs Strutt would return unexpectedly with a five-piece jazz combo and a tray of mince pies.

'When Daddy was alive we always did home entertainments on Boxing Day. Each took a turn and did something. I've been practising some new pieces for descant recorder. What will you do?'

'Not me. I'm not a performer.'

'Oh, but you must. That's the rule. What about a poem? Or a mime?'

'No. I don't think so.'

'Juggling? Card tricks? We've got a pack somewhere.'

'Quite honestly, Rosalind, I'd rather not. I'll just watch.'

'Not to worry. We'll think of something.'

They cleared the table together and while she searched for crumbs with the carpet-sweeper he snatched a piece of cold lamb. They washed and dried and put away everything concerned with the meal. He had never seen evidence disposed of so thoroughly. And, when the last spoon was back in its box, she set to and prepared for the afternoon's revelries. She set up her music-stand and checked the bookmark in her poetry book. The ill-gotten lamb was stuck half way down his gullet, reminding him that theft never pays, and when she started to limber up on the recorder he wished he had not been so hasty in his condemnation of Twice Nightly Tufnell.

'I'm going to begin with two pieces that you're sure to know. "Galliard St Thomas Wake", and then "Where Griping Grief". Two, three . . .'

80

He tapped along appreciatively. The pieces didn't last long. Then she primed the record player and put on some Vaughan Williams for atmosphere and read 'Pelleas and Ettarre' from Tennyson's *Idylls of the King*. It went on and on. There were a lot of damsels and donjons and she seemed to have some difficulty knowing when to breathe. He was worried about spotting when to applaud. And no wonder. The last line, when it came, was 'And Modred thought the time is hard at hand', which left a number of loose ends, but Rosalind had planned ahead and spared him any confusion by bowing very deeply and putting the book down.

'Are you sure you won't do a card trick, Filbert?'

'No. Truly.'

'Well, now for a change of mood. Two more pieces for recorder and then we'll dance the Gay Gordons.'

This had always been the trouble with Didge. He would cross bridges before he had to. He had seen the Gay Gordons danced when he was a boy, so he knew it was a dance in which enthusiasm counted for at least as much as technique. But because he had never actually danced it, and because it involved arms and legs functioning separately he plunged into mouthwatering panic and he had no chance of noticing that as recorder tunes go, 'Buffalo Gals' and 'Dere's someone in de house wid Dinah' were real winners.

And he needn't have worried. Rosalind took total charge of him, up and down the room, round and back again. By the time the music ended they had nearly caught up with it and Didge was enjoying himself.

'You're very good, Filbert. Really quite good.'

'I'm a bit heavy, that's the only thing.'

'Yes, you are. But you were still very good. Did you dance a lot when you were young?'

'Not at all. There was always too much to do at home. Hutches to clean out. Punctures to repair.'

'But at university. I'm sure you danced a lot there. I can

imagine you were very much in demand. I wasn't. I've always put it down to being an only child. I could drink as much as three glasses of sherry and still not feel able to take part in a limbo competition.'

'You seem very accomplished to me, Rosalind. Widely read. Musical . . .'

'There's no store put by that. Not these days. One needs to know how to sniff things. How to start a car without a key. We never learned things like that at St Hilda's. We did the quick-step. Can I ask you something, Filbert? Something personal?'

He had been wondering whether hypothermia was a painful death.

'Tell me honestly, Filbert. Do you think I can wear oatmeal?'

'Well . . . it's a very nice get-up you've got on today.'

'I've always worn a lot of oatmeal. And sometimes I just wonder. Sometimes, Filbert, I think I'll turn the world upside down and buy a pair of trousers.'

'You could do.'

'I don't know. It's easy for men to say these things. I'm forty-seven and there are steps I've never taken. Never danced till dawn. Gone out without a cardigan.'

'No reason why you shouldn't, Rosalind. I have every con-fidence in you. Why shouldn't you wear trousers?'

'Because trousers might only be the start of it. They might lead to things.'

'Things?'

'What if I ended up having my ears pierced and just walking away? Just walking away in a straight line and keeping going.'

'Nobody would mind.'

'But what about my pension? What about if the world turns out to be flat?'

'You'd be all right. In trousers.'

She relented and turned on one bar of the fire. She had something special for the rest of the afternoon she said. It was her much-acclaimed slide show on the Marriage-Resisters of

Antwerp. He let the pictures pass before him. Pleasant, plain little rooms. Water-lilies in walled gardens. One of the coach driver that shouldn't really have got into the box.

At home there would be a pot of tea brewing ready for the final of 'Celebrity Legs', and Hedley would be trying to shell nuts. There was a nice shot of the herb garden. They had, she said, come to a sticky end, burned alive to promote the inquisitional cause. He wondered what was for tea and whether there was a telly anywhere in the house.

It was six before they wrapped up the Marriage-Resisters. Rosalind put on the lights and offered to get out her recorder again and play 'Eccles Maggot', but somehow the moment had passed. He would have liked Mrs Strutt to come back so he could have some more gin and talk to her about everything. Even about what had happened to him in the back of that Fantasia hatchback. But he could feel Boxing Day slipping away from him. They sat in silence. He retraced Celia's last steps. Rosalind wondered what the Marriage-Resisters would have thought of trousers. And when they noticed each other again it was still Christmas, so she fetched another cracker each and they shared a Pot Noodle, to take up the slack in the conversation.

Chapter 12

Sleet blew against the front of the house all night and he woke, every hour on the hour. When the alarm clock buzzed at seven he was deeply asleep. He wanted to stay in bed for ever with his feet tucked into the hole in the blanket and one hand down the front of his pyjama trousers. He felt in the dark for his dressing-gown and found a jumper.

Downstairs the ashes were stone cold. He put the kettle on and sat close to the electric fire watching Hereward Cable, until his trouser leg scorched and he felt moved to look at the weather. When he opened the door, the cat appeared, weaving and whining, desperate to be in.

It pushed through his legs, paddled two circuits of the front hall and relieved itself extravagantly on the sisal mat.

He sucked the hot tea through his teeth and thought. The first day back after Christmas. They would be bored mindless. On the loose for a month, three weeks for pleasure and one for burst pipes, cruising round Kettering, stealing things they didn't need, frightening people who were frightened already. And now back to the Annexe. It would take every trick in the book to get them to sit down and have a meaningful learning experience.

He dressed downstairs and searched the cubby-hole for his waterproof cape. He found eleven old tins of boot polish and a clothes airer that fell on his head. But no waterproof. He put on his bike clips, pulled up his collar and was on his way out when he remembered and went back to write across the top of Daddo's *Tit-Bits:* BUY SUGAR. P.S. USED DISHRAG FOR CAT SHIT.

84

Glenda was at her gate with a shovel, ready to see off any weather that might try to settle. And all across the town those who had work to go to leaned into the January morning and never looked up.

The decorations should come down. That was the first thing. He only suggested it. There was nothing insistent in his voice. But to see the way they carried on you'd have thought they were under threat of execution. Lee-Anne and Jacqui threw themselves at the foot of the Christmas tree, foaming at the mouth. Nikki went into premature labour. And Terri lay down and set about herself to save the others the bother. Didge was exasperated.

'All right, all right, all right. I only said it was getting on into January and we ought to think about it. That's all. When I was a boy it all had to be packed away by Twelfth Night. All right. One more day. You can leave it like this for one more day and then it will have to go. Now do you understand?'

'Why can't it stop up? For ever.'

'Because, Aspen, it wouldn't be special if it was there all the time. Seasons come and seasons go. And once Christmas has gone there's nothing worse than tinsel.'

They started up again. After he'd talked Lindy down from the noose she'd made from the fairylight flex, he soothed them back to their seats.

'Listen. How would you like it if we decorated the room for the next big festival?'

That went down quite well.

'How would it be if we decorated the Annexe for Easter?'

'Is that tomorrow?'

'Not quite.'

'Is it the day after tomorrow?'

'No. It's in the spring. It'll be just before you leave school.'

But they wanted something sooner than that. Easter was years away. They made him get out his diary.

85

He suggested Greek Independence Day, or St David's Day, but they couldn't see the point. Mandy wanted to trim up for the 425th anniversary of the death of Ivan the Terrible but it still wasn't really soon enough. In the end, just for peace, Didge settled for Abraham Lincoln's birthday and let them think about a colour scheme. They weren't very clear about who Lincoln had been, though he went through it several times, but he thought that eventually they'd see that there didn't have to be balloons.

After lunch he got Michelle to take him to Secure Stores. She was calm and sure-footed, holding his hand when he was nervous about turning corners. And she was patient. She sat on Chitty's lap once she'd finished her own shopping, and didn't try to hurry him when he wanted to look and look at all the coloured paper and the pencils that hadn't been chewed.

They returned like hunters. Michelle went ahead with the glue-sticks and he followed her, cradling the lovely paper against the wind.

By two o'clock it was plain that it would get no lighter that day. The lamps stayed on all afternoon and the floor was gradually covered with red and blue paper, gluey and done for, and deformed white stars. They were not a lot nearer to celebrating the spirit of America.

Then Rosalind popped in. She said things like 'An Art lesson. How jolly!' and 'Gosh, don't Christmas things brighten a late January afternoon!' and was too matey by half until he asked after Mrs Strutt, and she froze him with her tiny eyes.

'She's quite well. Considering.'

'Not ill I hope?'

'Not for want of trying.'

'Oh dear.'

'And you certainly made a big hit. She took to you in a big way. But that's Mummy. All or nothing. Until she turns. Then she can be very nasty.'

86

'It was very nice to meet her. She was really very nice to me. I mean it was a very nice day all round. I've been intending to drop you a line. To say thanks. But you know how it is . . .'

'Don't give it another thought. I'm only glad you don't have to endure what I have to.'

'Oh Rosalind. Please, tell me about it. Girls, I'm quite certain I said you could go.'

Only Jacqui and Lindy were left, standing in the ruins of an afternoon of papercraft. They were interested in Rosalind's sheepskin boots and in her closeness to tears.

'Holidays are never easy with families. Thrown into each other's company. Daddo and I have our moments, believe you me.'

'But your father's not a deceitful, ungrateful man, Filbert. I'm sure of that. If you do something for his own good he doesn't hurl it back in your face. Women are different. They can turn suddenly. They can be very nasty. And sly.'

'So what happened?'

'She's been wriggling out of things again. Wriggling out of what's best for her.'

'Wriggling?'

'Out of Spain.'

'Spain?'

'I tried to send her to Spain. For the winter.'

'What a lovely idea.'

'Of course it was. But Mummy thought differently. Wriggled away after she'd gone through passport control. And that's not all.'

'No?'

'No. She took others with her. Talked others into throwing away six weeks on the Costa Blanca. And of course I feel responsible for the whole business. Mummy was the ring-leader.'

'Perhaps she'd rather stay in England.'

'Perhaps she would. But if she thinks I'm going to allow her to spend the winter in England, sitting around, dying of the cold, she must think I'm a very strange daughter indeed.'

'But if she wrapped up well. Daddo seems to get by.'

'Yes? Well, if that's a risk you're prepared to take. I'm pleased to see the girls are taking an interest in Art.'

'Yes. We're trying to develop an American theme. Stars are so hard to do free-hand though.'

'The main thing is that they want to do it.'

'Absolutely. So your mother's back in Kettering?'

'Yes. I've locked her stick away and bought her a tapestry cushion to work on. Are you going now? Your friends were waiting for you I noticed.'

Boyle and Nutts were standing proprietorially beside Didge's padlocked bike. Nutts had a parcel. Rosalind left him and walked on to her car. He hoped she hadn't seen them squeezing his arm and saying ManPower.

'You coming then?'

'Sorry?'

'To the gathering?'

'Sorry?'

'You coming to the gathering?'

'Well . . .'

'Corrigan wants to know.'

'Well, when is it?'

'Tonight.'

'It's very short notice.'

'We got a uniform for you.'

Nutts gave him the bundle.

'It's just that it'd be a bit of a rush tonight. I've got lessons to prepare for tomorrow. And the teatowels need a good boiling. I'd be a bit pushed.'

'Corrigan's expecting you.'

'He sent the gear.'

88

'It might not fit of course. I always have trouble with off-the-peg. I'm very short in the body. And long in the leg.'

'Ashby Street Scout Hut. Eight o'clock.'

'I'm not making any promises. None at all. My evenings are very busy. I'll certainly pop along one of the evenings. Have a word with Terence. Let him know how sorry we all are. But I don't know about tonight.'

They both squeezed him again and stood over him, breathing heavily, while he put the uniform in his saddle-bag and tried to unlock his bike with shaking hands.

He rode home and thought about Bella Strutt. And Art. Rosalind might have something. Good old Art might fill a few afternoons until the sun shone again. Glenda came out to check that her shovel was still there and saw him taking the uniform out of his bag.

'I see you've got your gear then?'

'I'm looking after it for a friend.'

'That'll need altering. That'll need taking up in the jacket and letting down in the leg.'

'It's all right, Glenda. It's not for me.'

'All right then. Your Dad's never salted his path all day.'

She followed him along the fence as he made for the back of the house. Daddo was in his slippers trying to unpeg the blue lacy briefs that were stiff and cold on the line.

'Hello, son.'

'Whose are the knickers?'

'I was just fetching them in for Glenda, son. Hed must have had them off her line. I'll knock them through again, Glen. Just in case. He might have done something with them.'

Glenda's eyes never left Didge's bundle.

'Had a nice day, son?'

They went in to where it was bright and warm and left Glenda and her shovel leaning against the fence.

'Don't forget,' she called. 'Drop it in and I'll put a tuck in it.'

Chapter 13

It was the first Thursday in the month. The library was open
and Tufnell would be visiting at home, monopolising the fire
and putting people off their food. The time had come for the
Easter Leavers to become visually aware, and for Didge to
prepare the way. He thought he'd call it Looking at Pictures.
Keep the word Art out of it. It would be for the best. He had
noticed that Art made Rosalind's lips wet.

He had hoped for a radiator but they were all taken.
Colonised by pinched and ragged people. Some of them were
eating. Some were rolling up smokes. Many of them were
absorbed in the library's most precious volumes, filling in all
the o's and the a's with fibre-tip pens. It had become
impossible to get dependable staff.

Didge reached down the *Bumper Book of World Art* and sat
in a cold, unsought place. He had no sooner turned to the
treasures of Assyria and Babylon than a man with foul breath
pulled up a chair and sat so close that their knees pressed
together. He offered Didge a Fisherman's Friend and leaned
forwards confidentially.

'Are you interested in Art at all?'

'Hm?'

'Art. Are you interested in it, by any chance?'

'Not especially.'

'I am.'

'Oh yes?'

'Yes. Know anything about the operatic works of Giuseppe
Verdi?'

'No.'

'I do.'

'That's nice.'

He whistled a bit from *Il Trovatore*, Act II.

'Care for Great Literature do you?'

'Pardon?'

'Great Literature. I was wondering whether you cared for it.'

'Yes. Yes, I suppose I do.'

'I thought so. I expect you'll have read all of the Classics?'

'Some of them.'

'I expect you know the whole of the Hardy canon.'

'I have read some Hardy.'

'Question! Who was the hunchback shopkeeper in *Desperate Measures*?'

'I don't think Thomas Hardy wrote that.'

'Correct! Nor did he pen *The Strange Tale of Monty McKenzie*.'

'No?'

'No.'

'Why mention them then?'

'Because they were written by Tony Hardy. That's my point. You sure you're not interested in Art?'

'Quite sure.'

'That's a shame. I've got a nice Oates I could show you.'

'An Oates?'

'Yes.'

'An original?'

'In the style of. Care to see it?'

'I'm rather busy. I'm a teacher you see.'

'Keeping warm until you can go home are you?'

'Certainly not. I'm devising a new syllabus component for the upper school. I have research to do. A great deal of research.'

'You must be an important man then.'

'Just a man with a deadline to meet. So I must get on.'

'I'll just sit with you then. It'd be a great honour to sit with such a busy important man. While he keeps warm until he can go home.'

'Will you please go away.'

'Of course. Of course. Say no more. I'll just show you the Oates and then I'll be on my way.'

He stood up, took off his jacket, lowered his braces and prepared to undo his fly. The girl behind the Loans Counter raised her arm, trying to catch his eye. He was obviously a regular. In there day after day pestering people.

It was, admittedly, a fine study in the style of Oates. The Battle of Trafalgar. On his left buttock the flagship *Victory* was depicted in close detail. And on the right the enemy fleet was drawn up under the steely command of Admiral Ville-neuve.

The girl from Loans ran across and tugged the trousers half way up the mast of the *Marie-Christine*.

'Mr Hardy! Mr Hardy!'

'What is it, Gillian? I'm busy.'

'It's your wife, Mr Hardy. She's in Non-Fiction Reserves and she wants to know if chops will be all right.'

'You should have said. Thank you, Gillian. Show her to my office.'

He rearranged his clothing and disappeared behind the door marked Principal Librarian. Gillian smiled, full of importance.

'It is a lovely picture isn't it?'

'Yes. Yes it is.'

'He's got the Battle of Jutland on his chest.'

Didge moved into the seclusion of Mythology and bided his time. In half an hour Tufnell would be gone and he could go home with the *Treasures of Florence* and the *French Impressionists*.

As he left there was a familiar figure lurking. Corrigan.

'Terence!'

92

Corrigan prodded him with a Large Print Edition of *Power Tool Carpentry*.

'Hello, Filbert. I've been waiting for you.'

'Hello, Terence. I've been wondering how you were getting on.'

'Have you, Filbert? That's nice. We've been expecting you.'

'I sent a note. After Celia. How are . . . things?'

'Mustn't grumble, Filbert. I've been putting new laminated working surfaces in the kitchen. They've been a bit of a nightmare. Can't complain otherwise.'

'Celia was a terrible shock. Terrible. If only there was something we could have done.'

'We've been expecting you to come, Filbert. With you having the free use of a uniform. It was the least we expected.'

'I do mean to drop in, Terence. But I've been very tied up.'

'Your uniform's ready for you. It's been let out.'

'Yes?'

'So we'll expect you tomorrow night.'

After Corrigan had gone, Didge shook alone against the wall for a while, and then went round in the rotating door three times before he bothered to try and get out.

A number seven stopped in Silver Street. He could easily have caught it. But the people on it were looking at him. He detoured through Chatham Street and Market Hill, keeping away from gloomy doorways and trying not to step on any cracks in the pavement. The sky above Cavendish Street tried to snow on him. The wind blew grit in his eyes. And in the paper shop Gerald wouldn't look at him straight when he asked the price of a crossword book.

Hedley was sitting too close to the television watching a special News Bulletin. Live coverage. Reporters were protesting their loss for words with such fluency that you couldn't even hear their lapse into horrified silence. Right there, in his own house, while he still quivered from Corrigan, Berkshire

93

burned. Wimmin were cutting a swathe through the Home Counties. From Windsor Great Park they were sweeping unstoppable into Hampshire. There were pockets holding out. In Aldershot and Bisley there were still Army wives who knew what was what. But in Winkfield the sky was orange. And in Sunningdale men had come home from important business to find their golf-bags vandalised and hostess-trolleys lying wrecked on the grass verges.

The quivering stopped and he was violently sick in the sink. Hedley came and helped him rinse his face with cold water and unblock the plughole. That was when it hit him how really bad things were. There was carrot in it. And Didge never ate carrot. Never.

Chapter 14

He wouldn't have gone. He wasn't that bothered by Corrigan. And even though Glenda had done something clever with the grey cotton drill and thrown in Carl's discarded Union Jack neckerchief out of neighbourliness, he still wouldn't have gone. But Tufnell had arrived and, as their local agent for New Dimensions Marital Aids, was setting up his props for a Marketing Party. And Daddo said he didn't want Didge around making his friends feel ill at ease. Hedley was going to be allowed. Even though he was bound to drink too much fizzy pop. And Didge was older than him. But Daddo wouldn't be swayed. It was quite a nice evening for going out, anyway. For the time of year.

It was the being new he hated. Being asked to help stack the chairs at the end. Or make the tea. And not knowing how much tea to put in the pot, or how to light the gas. This sort of thing had hampered his social life.

There were a lot of grey men making for the scout hut. And Nutts was on the door. Didge pretended to know him terrifically well, and then tried to mingle, self-conscious with no pockets for his hands.

Corrigan was clearly a very important man. He was the only one with armbands and a peaked cap. He was dealing in a distracted unseeing way with a man in shorts and a whistle.

They started on the stroke of eight, with 'God Save the King', in wobbly ranks. They stood to attention while a man with a very straight back told them that the growing menace was at their very doors and firesides, and that ManPower in North London had closed a Wimmin's Centre and two girls' schools in the last month alone. An unnamed party was commended for domestic bravery and a roll of honour was recited for the ManPower members who had fallen victims of Tarporley and Nantwich Wimmin's Institute and were now listed Missing, presumed casseroled.

They did running on the spot, sit-ups, push-ups, squat-thrusts and scissor-jumps, and Didge's pulse rate rose until he was beyond caring. He was just glad of the glass of cold milk and a chance to sit on his mat with a fig roll until his heart could be trusted again and it was time for Mental Hygiene.

A life-sized cardboard figure was propped on a chair at one end of the hut, and Corrigan stood beside it with a pointing stick. It was supposed to be a woman. You could tell that. It had an apron tied over its biology. And when Corrigan pulled aside the cover and began 'Wimmin . . .' Didge gasped and looked at it just a little at a time.

So wimmin were different. And that was what Mother must have looked like. Not even a belly-button.

'Wimmin. Know your enemy. Know her well. Know what she's hiding under her pinny.'

'Not a thing,' Didge whispered to the man on the next mat, but he got shushed, and for the next hour he sat transfixed by the many things he had wondered about and never dared to ask.

Corrigan told them all he knew, but he returned again and again to the point that there were many things about wimmin that could not be explained. Important parts of them were invisible. That was something Didge hadn't appreciated. They had the internal means of squeezing the very life out of a man, squeezing it out to the last drop. They could bleed for days on end, and regularly did, and at the end of it all, instead of being dead they were fitter than ever. They could wash and iron six pairs of curtains, re-stock a deep-freeze with meat pies and still have the energy to deprive a man of his sleep. It was clear enough. Wimmin were unnatural.

96

Didge remembered how his mother had darned socks till the cows came home. And creosoted fences. Small wonder Daddo needed his bed so much these days.

And Rosalind. Did she have an apron under her frock? And hidden structures? It prayed on his mind.

They finished with songs. 'Men Be Stalwart Men Be True' and 'Never Let A Woman Get On Top', and then they all linked hands and vowed allegiance to ManPower and to Him whenever He might come.

Daddo still had a houseful when he got home. All in the front-room. Chesney and Simpson and Dickie Deadlegs and all the allotment crowd. Hed was in the kitchen eating crisps, but the men were watching Tufnell demonstrating a battery-operated rubber device called I'll Be Buggered.

Daddo said, 'Hello, son. How about one of these?' and passed him a single glove. It had an unusual texture on the palm that made him feel ashamed to have touched it.

'Feels nice, don't it, son? That's called Lonely Nites. Feel it again. I'm ordering you one of them. For your birthday.'

Tufnell was just finishing. They all watched while he deflated the Dusky Temptress and folded her away in her box. And then they turned their attention to Didge and admired his uniform. That pleased Daddo. As he showed them to the door one by one, he said things like 'He's a very good son really' and 'I'd have joined up myself but I'd never pass the medical'.

Tufnell was the last to go. Hedley bobbed about helping him with his boxes, insisting that he didn't need the toilet, and Twice Nightly slipped a pair of red satin Skimpy Knicks into Didge's hand and winked at him with insufferable intimacy.

'You can have these for your lady friend,' he whispered, 'her with the moustache.'

Chapter 15

Rosalind was making an effort.

Following the instructions in an article called 'Ringing the Changes with Powder and Paint', she had crept out to Magnadrug and crept home again with a lighter purse and a secret parcel up the sleeve of her coat. The stairs creaked. But Bella was shut away in the breakfast-room pretending not to be interested. In her room Rosalind pushed a chair under the doorhandle, then sat in front of her mirror with her coat on and said several times:

'So . . . let's make a start.'

She stayed there right through lunch time, daring her mother to call her to table and notice the eyeshadow. Bella had gone her own way, though, with a bar of chocolate and an apple, closing the front door quietly as she went out.

By five she had tried Sweetly Simple, Come Hither, and Rainbow Explosion, and had practised saying, 'There's nothing remarkable about a woman making the best of herself' with each new look. She had just compromised with ice-blue eyelids and a discreet fluff of Calypso Carib on her cheeks, when Bella called her from the foot of the stairs.

'Ros. I'm just burning some toast. Should you like some?' She was hungry. And the time had come. She wavered for a moment with a pad of moist cotton-wool in her hand, and then, with rare courage, went down to face it out. Bella's coat lay on the bottom step where she had dropped it. Rosalind hung it up and took a last look in the mirror on the coat-stand. It was certainly a very blue sort of blue. She screwed up her face to help the whole business bed down and steadied herself for Mummy.

Mummy was reading Gloria Steinem, with a margarine tub on the table. She ate four slices of toast, an orange and a bag of peanuts and never looked up once.

'I think I might go to America in the autumn.'

'What do you mean?'

'New York. In September.'

'What on earth for?'

'Just to go. I've never been.'

'But you're old.'

'There are old people who live in New York. I'm not that old.'

'What about your hip?'

'I'll take it with me.'

'What about getting mugged?'

'There's no need to arrange it in advance. It either happens to you or it doesn't.'

'You won't know anyone.'

'I shall by the time I come back.'

'Why not give Harrogate another chance?'

'I want to go to New York. Everyone says it's hell on earth.'

'You've knocked orange peel on the floor.'

'Hell on earth. I shall be able to eat in the street. And ride on all those little ferries. All that dirty water. And yell at people.'

'You'll get murdered.'

'I shan't. I shall behave so oddly that everyone will think I might murder them. Anyway, I have to die somewhere. I can't see it matters where.'

'You could have gone to Spain to die but you wouldn't. And you ought to be thinking about having your sinuses done in September.'

'Hell on earth. I wonder if it is. Kettering is hell on earth. Have a peanut.'

Now she looked. When Rosalind was wrestling with her selfish insistence on having her throat cut in Brooklyn and had forgotten all about her face.

'Do you mind if I say something, darling? Powdered blusher isn't a good idea. Not on a downy complexion like yours. It sort of sits on top and screams at people. Try my Cremestik Shaper. Any time you like. Do have a nut.'

So Rosalind stuck with the ice-blue eyes and the Calypso Carib because Bella was clearly in a rage about not being allowed to go to New York to get raped and was getting her own back by lying about cosmetics. And that was why she was looking so blue and orange when she dropped in to the Annexe to get a snap reaction from Didge and caught him red-handed with Art.

He had shown them some Turners and some Corots. Dead boring they said. And could they have a go on the sunbed? He showed them Caravaggio, and Kandy and Michelle started frigging around with Lindy's chain-saw.

It was Poussin's 'Rape of the Sabine Women' that focused them. Mandy noticed there was a woman in the middle of the picture who definitely wasn't being raped. Whatever the chap had suggested, she was definitely going along with it. To the extent that she was pointing out a quiet corner away from all that rape and pillage where they could talk over things of mutual interest. Her and the Pink Plunger. Definitely. But it was Goya who clinched it. Him and Velásquez and all that Spanish royalty. Eighteen Plus Remedial exploded. They loved it. They were unanimous. Goya had been taking the piss.

They stalked Didge, laughing till they ached, crossing their eyes, sticking their tongues out, pretending to be dimly lit, overbred Spanish Infantas. Then Rosalind arrived. After that it was downhill all the way. She sat in his chair while they cheered for Jackson Pollock. She leaned over the back of it while they went quiet for Magritte. And when they'd packed away and gone home, flushed and withdrawn over Otto Dix, she stood against the outer door and Didge said,

100

'You're looking very . . . nice.'

Tufnell delivered the Lonely Nites Velvi Gluv after tea. And
Glenda came in. She'd been spring cleaning. She dropped a
sad little box on the couch and said that, if Didge could use
any of it, he was welcome, for none of her lads would ever
darken her door again. Carl's dog-eared *Path to Racial Purity*.
Brett's attainment badges from when he was a cadet in Youths
of Albion: Woodcraft, Advanced Woodcraft, and Abstention
from Self-Abuse. And a penknife that wouldn't open.

Didge sat all evening with one foot dead beneath him,
reading the instructions that had come with the Velvi Gluv and
remembering what Corrigan had said about wimmin. He
didn't think about Rosalind. He was careful of that. But he
thought around her. He wondered whether what Corrigan
had said was true of absolutely all wimmin. Whether there
might not be some who were just the same as him under their
aprons. And he wondered why Manet's 'Luncheon on the
Grass' with the bare lady was missing from his class file.

Barbie had only borrowed it because she was interested in how
they done things in olden days. She had meant to return it first
thing the next morning, but, as things turned out, she missed
the next day, and Didge had a visitor waiting for him when he
bundled into the Annexe just before nine.

'Haven't they bloody well pensioned you off yet?'

'I'm sorry?'

'I said it was about time they let you go.'

Eighteen years on there had been no improvement. The skin
was tired. And under it everything had moved a little.
Downwards. But there was no mistaking her. It was Diane.
Dirty Diane. Diane who had had a hand in turning Swills
nasty. Diane who had blooded Didge in his probationary year
and now stood before him with Manet's *Luncheon on the
Grass*.

'I wondered where that had got to.'

'I bet you bloody did.'

'Where did you get it?'

'Up my girl's jumper. I'll get you struck off.'

'And your girl is . . . ?'

'My girl is at home looking after the babby and learning something useful. I'm getting her in somewhere better.'

'It was just Art, you see.'

'Fuck Art.'

'Fine, fine.'

'I shall have you banned. Banned from everywhere. And him.'

'Him?'

'Him who took this.'

'It's not a photograph. It's a painting. Quite old.'

'I shall still get him banned. You should check them before they leave here.'

'Check them?'

'Every night. Check what they've got up their jumpers. I should like to see you strung up. Anyhow, Barbie's finished. She's not coming back here. I'm not risking it.'

Barbie. Of course. Dirty Diane of the Boiler Room. Who had been pollinated by Whiffer and Tosh and Guffy and Gumboil and many, many others, and had begat Barbie. Barbie's mother was an Old Girl. And now Barbie was an Old Girl. Time was cracking on.

Chapter 16

Daddo and Hedley wanted the 'Best of Bonanza' but Didge couldn't be bothered. Eventually he took the fan-heater and went upstairs to do a crossword.

The police and the military were busy that night. When he looked out of the window there were no wimmin in sight but he could hear them calling across the streets and away to the west something was burning. He was stumped for seventeen across, with biro leaking on his hands and his eye wandering to the unused Velvi Gluv, when there was the rap of a stone on his window and a long low whistle. He put down his book and put out the light. He peered sideways into the empty street. A little snow had begun to fall. Another stone hit the pane nearest to him and then the light of a torch began to dance right below where he stood. It must be wimmin. Come to torment him. Or ManPower. On covert activities. He loosed the catch on the window very slowly and sank to his knees. He was too low now to see the movement of the torch, but he could hear someone down there, thinking. There were no more stones. No more whistles. For a moment just two tensed bodies. And then a voice from the garden.

'Filbert. Filbert. Can you hear me?'

He let the window swing open a little more but kept his head down.

'Who is it?'

'A friend. Listen carefully and answer quietly. Can you get out of the house without being seen?'

'Yes, but . . .'

'Then come down quickly. Don't say any more. Just shut the window and come down.'

He did exactly as he was told. He closed the window and went down in his shirt-sleeves, leaving his bottom dentures soaking in the tumbler of Zing.

Behind the living-room door 'Tough Bastards' was just starting. Daddo and Hed would be snug for another hour. Outside he couldn't see a thing. He strained his eyes to see what was in the bushes and jumped when the voice came from right by his side.

'Filbert, I think you need help.'

It was Rosalind's Mummy.

'Mrs Strutt!'

'Bella. Follow me.'

There was no one to see them. Not even Glenda. His mind began to clear. He was in the street with Bella Strutt. She was all in black and inviting him to get astride her Fijio 1000. When he hesitated, she mistook his fear for cold and unzipped her leather jacket. She put it round his shoulders.

'No, no. You need it.'

'I'm all right. I've got another three layers under here. See if you can squeeze into it.'

'Where are we going?'

'No questions. Are you on?'

'Do I have to lean when we go round a bend or anything?'

'Hell no! Just hold on!'

She took him away from the town and the sirens. His ears ached. His mouth and hands were numb. He was having the time of his life.

They stopped just beyond Barton Seagrave at a solitary house. There were cars parked in the long drive but the house was dark. She took his hand and let him through a side-door into a passage that smelled of beer. He was pulled after her, feeling for the wall, feeling for steps. She opened a door in front of

104

them and he fell behind her into a warm, comfortable kitchen.

'Where are we? Where on earth are we?'

'Not far. I'll have you home in ten minutes. This is one of our Safe Houses.'

'Is it? What's it for?'

'For being safe in.'

'You're not living here?'

'Not yet. Some of us are.'

'Do they need to hide or something?'

'Don't we all?'

'I don't know. Do we?'

'Filbert, listen to Bella.'

'Yes?'

'You have a class full of girls. Big girls.'

'Yes.'

'And you're with ManPower.'

'Yes.'

'And what are ManPower planning?'

'We're going away on manoeuvres soon. Camping.'

'Yes. Yes. But in the long term.'

'The long term?'

'In the long term, darling, ManPower is bent on destroying wimmin. The Clearances. And they'll start with the young ones. The breeders.'

'Breeders?'

'Yes. And they'll use you, Filbert. Because of your big girls. You'll be part of it.'

'They haven't mentioned it.'

'You don't listen. You're not in the Boys' Brigade now, sweetheart. You're in with the men. And they're after your girls.'

'Where will they want to take them?'

'They won't take them anywhere. Well, the Hunky Meat Pie Factory, possibly. Certainly no further. Unless we do something.'

'What can we do?'

'We can spirit a few away.'

'Yes?'

'I have a friend. A business woman. She'll take some of them. Overseas. To work overseas.'

'Overseas? Work? But that's wonderful. Does she have any openings for men?'

'She'll only take some of them. Ones that are strong. And clean.'

'I can clean them up. What type of work will it be?'

'Service industries. Entertainment. That sort of thing. But she can't take them all. You must understand that. The rest will have to take their chance.'

'It's very good of you to bother.'

'There are thousands of them, Filbert. They're paltry specimens but they're tomorrow's wimmin. And something has to be salvaged. We're trying to spread it around. A little here. A little there. And this is your little bit. She'll contact you. She'll tell you what to do. And now I must get you back before you're missed.'

'Does Rosalind know?'

'Filbert. Dear boy. Rosalind knows nothing.'

'Does she know you're here?'

'I'm not here. I'm at Mothers' Union.'

'What shall I tell her?'

'Tell her?'

'Rosalind.'

'Tell her to throw away that blue eyeshadow.'

She delivered him to the end of the road and he returned her jacket. When Daddo heard him in the kitchen he called to him to bring the Jaffa Cakes, and while they drank their malted milk they were so caught up with the Pro-Am Pistol Shooting that no one noticed his slippers were covered in snow.

106

Chapter 17

The Honourable Member for Northamptonshire North was seeing to a little constituency business. It was his turn for the desk but Gribbins was still slumped across it asleep. It was his turn for Nina as well, so he got her to help him lift Gribbins and resettle him against Hogshaw's shopping trolley.

He looked through his messages. It was a typical trayful. Whining entreaties for re-housing from arthritic sluggards in highrise flats. Petulant carping about food shortages from the mothers of young brats. And the usual invitations. Requests for money. Threats of assassination. And a note that mystified him: *Sorry to have missed you on Boxing Day but looking forward to seeing you Wednesday. Kind regards, Rosalind.*

He checked the envelope to be sure he hadn't picked up any of Gribbins's droppings, but it was clearly addressed to John Ryder Knight MP.

'Nina, do we know a Rosalind?'

'Say again?'

'Rosalind. Does the name mean anything?'

'Can I get back to you on that one, RK? I'll have to check the files.'

'Fine. Just wondering whether to expect trouble.'

'Will do.'

He worked his way through the day's voting list, ticking the boxes that Nina had underlined. There was the slightly contentious Prohibition of French Cheeses (Consolidation) Act, but otherwise nothing of note. The Ecclesiastical Appellate Proceedings statute would go through on the tick. Nina came in with some papers for him to sign and brought the Paternity File with her.

'We have a Roxanne. And a Belinda. But no Rosalind.'

'That's odd.'

'Is there a problem?'

'Probably not. It's just this note.'

'Have you ever been married to a Rosalind?'

'I don't think so.'

'No daughter of that name?'

'Not that I've admitted to.'

'I'd ignore it. Your party is just going through Security. They'll be ready for you in ten minutes.'

'Party?'

'Freshfields Comprehensive, Kettering. You agreed to talk to them.'

'I did?'

'I have the letters here. One from a Mr Didge giving details of the size of the class, time of arrival and so on. And another from a Miss Strutt, Senior Mistress, reminding you of family connections. Her grandmother was one of the Warwickshire Willeys and she says you're sure to remember . . .'

'I've got to see these people have I?'

'Yes. You're to go down to reception in five minutes and greet them pleasantly.'

'Is there anyone here to advise me?'

'It won't be necessary. According to Mr Didge they're eighteen-year-old girls of very limited intelligence.'

'I usually see someone from the Ministry before I talk to anyone. Are you sure there's nothing laid on?'

'No, really. Just tell them about the Mother of Parliaments. Mention Pym and Hampden . . .'

'Are they going to be there then?'

'Only in spirit. Tell them what a busy time an MP has of things, and pop them up here for a quick look at the nuts and bolts.'

108

'I see. Quite easy really.'
'Nothing to it.'
'And I meet them in . . . ?'
'Reception.'
'And that is . . . ?'
'The place where you come in.'
'Fine, fine. Off I go then.'

Didge was having a lot of trouble with the girls. Mandy and her mates kept slipping round to the back of the queue and Lee-Anne had three intimate body searches before he realised what she was doing. It would have been useful to have had Rosalind there whipping them in but she had excused herself at the very last moment. She said Mummy's back had gone, but he knew better. He had seen Bella that very morning. She had overtaken him on her new Kamikaze, poncho flying in the wind, and an easel strapped to the back. She had called out to him,
'Lovely day, Filbert. I'm off to paint some headless ducks.'
So he knew Rosalind was telling porkies. And he knew why. She had bought a trouser-suit, specially for the occasion. She'd worn it to school. And then she had bottled out. Rosalind Strutt had left him in the lurch because she was in a funk over the cut of her trousers.

They eyed each other across Constituency reception. Didge had never met an MP before and John Ryder Knight had never met anyone from the sharp end of his government's Extended Life Preparation Programme. He knew that it was one of those jobs. Like solid wastes disposal. It had to be done. But he preferred not to be reminded of the toll it must take. And here was Didge, bloated and blemished, his arms and legs failing to reach any sort of agreement with each other.
'Mr Ryder Knight!'
'Mr Didge? Mr Didge! And these must be your girls. I've been looking forward to meeting you all.'

109

'It's very good of you to spare the time. You must be a very busy man.'

'I am. I am. But you are the people that matter. I have you all in my care, and caring's the name of the game.'

'Rosalind was sorry not to be able to come at the last minute. She asked me to say . . .'

'Rosalind? Good grief! Has she been in touch with you as well? How much does she want?'

'Well she just asked me to say not to worry about Boxing Day and that she'll be in touch.'

'Boxing Day? I could have sworn that was Leonora. I must have had more vermouth than I thought. Well . . . this, as you can see, is reception. Where we meet people. And if you'd like to follow me I'll show you the innards of the machine. Where the graft gets done.'

They followed him along corridors, past running women and purposeful men.

'And do any of these bright young things have political ambition?'

'Too early to say yet. Most of them can barely speak.'

'That should never deter anyone. Not being able to speak is no bar. Caring. That's what counts. Heavens, we even have people from Warwick University. Caring. That's the bottom line. This is where I do my desk work. Nina, where were we on Boxing Day?'

'Reno, Nevada.'

'Ah yes. Who were we with?'

'Hal Halloran and the Way to Life Crusade.'

'Yes. Of course we were. And we've never heard him referred to as Rosalind?'

'No.'

'Fine, Nina. Now this is Mr Drudge from Flatfields Academy and these are his girls.'

A telephone rang and woke Gribbins.

110

'Visitors! Welcome! Welcome indeed!'

'My visitors, Gribbins.'

'As you say, as you say. And any visitors of yours are visitors of mine. Gribbins is the name. Member for Northamptonshire South for seventeen years.'

'Didge, Freshfields Comprehensive.'

'Champion. And all these gorgeous girls? Searching for husbands I dare say. And why not . . . gorgeous. I hope you're glad to be here, girls. I am. Can you feel the throbbing dynamo of political power? I can. Don't move an inch. Stop and consider. What are we all doing here? How did it come about? Who made us this priceless gift? We owe them a moment of grateful reflection. And I'll say those thanks for us all. I thank Canning, and the Radical Philosophers. I thank the Women's Suffrage Union. I even thank the Chartists and that misguided man Keir Hardie.'

Ryder Knight looked round anxiously.

Didge wished Rosalind could have been there. Gribbins was a twenty-two carat tub-thumper. But Aspen was at his ear.

'Didge, Didge, where's the lav?'

'Listen to the man, Aspen.'

'I'm bursting for a pee.'

'Listen for the peroration.'

Halfway through the Jarrow March, Nina showed them into the Hospitality Room for orangeade, and Didge grasped the moment to ask Ryder Knight about the cut and thrust of parliamentary debate.

'Never touch the stuff.'

'No debates?'

'Very few do. Only the incurables. Gribbins shuffles along for a bit of a spout from time to time.'

'So how do you decide how to vote?'

'Prime Minister tells us.'

'But some of it must need discussing. And amendments. That sort of thing.'

111

'I believe he chews things over with his secretary. And his mother. Gets the feel of public opinion. From the window-cleaner. And people. And then he decides.'

'Just like that?'

'Yes. It saves heaps of time.'

'But I thought we talked things over in Britain. I thought that was one of the things that made us better than other places. Checks and balances. Isn't that what's kept the hordes from the gate all these years?'

'No, no, no. That's the old democracy trick you're thinking of. I've heard that one a few times. No, no, no. We have Government for the Nineties. It works awfully well.'

'And do you ever go into the chamber? Do you ever speak?'

'Heavens no! I'm far too busy. Making speeches never got the baby bathed. And anyway I'm a martyr to my nerves.'

When Didge came out into frail sunshine he felt well satisfied. There had been no bloodshed. No structural damage. And Kev's Vista Coach stood waiting for him with the girls already in their seats. He started a head count and was nearly ready to give Kev the go-ahead when there was a desperate banging on the outside of the coach and John Ryder Knight collapsed on the step unable to speak. It was the security man close behind him that brought the day to a standstill.

'You got a party with green knickers?'

'I beg your pardon?'

'Green knickers. With black lace. Name of Aspirin.'

'What do you mean?'

'There's been trouble. You're the Kettering mob.'

'Yes?'

'And you've left one of your little ladies behind.'

'I don't think so.'

'I know so. Green knickers. Name of Aspirin.'

'Aspen. Is Aspen here?'

She wasn't.

112

'What's happened? Is she hurt? I'll come with you.'

'No need. She's on her way to St George's. She's been took care of.'

'But what happened?'

'Gribbins. It happens from time to time. He's prone to it. That's why if I had my way we wouldn't have women in here. They should be kept out altogether.'

'What has he done to her?'

'She must have started him off. It takes two. Rigor coitus they call it. Locked together. He is prone, but she must have egged him on.'

'But what happens now?'

'They sort them out at St George's. They usually give him a calcium shot and then wait till they can separate them. He has very strong thigh muscles. He's got a vice-like grip.'

'And how did it happen?'

'She said he was helping her find a lav. I wouldn't have them in the building. There's always trouble.'

'Will they let me see her?'

'Not till they've got him off her. That wouldn't be very appropriate would it? Or am I very old-fashioned? No. If I was you I'd be off before I get you done for lingering in a restricted parking zone.'

Chapter 18

Didge sent Gemma with a note for Aspen's mother. It said there was no cause for concern and promised that he would visit before school the next day. Then he went home to have a migraine.

He wouldn't be coaxed out of it. Hedley tried with a gammon steak and a ring of pineapple, but by half past seven he was in bed with an extra pair of socks and a jug of soluble aspirin. He woke just after midnight thinking it must be morning, but the landing light was still on and Daddo was having one of his nightmares, calling out in anguish and thrashing about in his bed until it rocked the wall and made the coathangers dance in the wardrobe. Didge stuck his head under the pillow and wished he hadn't gone to bed so early.

First thing, he phoned St George's to find out when Aspen would be discharged and what the cost would be. She had remained, they said, chirpy almost to the end. She had endured the indignities with her chin up. And when Gribbins was prised free and immediately tried to mount a large Geordie charge-nurse called Titch, no one laughed louder or longer than that brave lass. But the shock to her system had been severe. Her electrolytes had gone to the dogs. Her kidneys had withdrawn their goodwill. And Aspen had slipped into unconsciousness and uncomplaining death.

Didge's mouth was dry. Monmouth Road had been too easy to find and now there was no more time to prepare for the terrible ordeal. He had never had to do such a thing before.

As his hand touched the gate, something stirred in the

114

overgrown hedge. It was on him before he could move out of range. Snarling and scratching in a confusion of black hair and rabid spittle, it ripped at the showerproof nylon of his sleeve. He had wit enough to protect his jugular, but the arm he raised against injury to his eyes was taken as a craven threat of violence, and the leaping, snapping creature worked itself into a passion of self-defence. Then, just as suddenly, it stopped. Felled, winded, by a shoe thrown from the front door step.

'Get down, Ashley. Get down. Get in.'

As it slunk sideways and untrusting past him and into the house, he realised why there was something familiar about the shape of the teeth. It was Aspen's younger brother. And the woman on the step with the other shoe in her hand was the woman he had come to see. Aspen's mother.

'Piss off.'

'I've come about . . .'

'Clear off else I'll set Vincent on you.'

From memory Vincent was the bigger one, so Didge knew he should act fast. He pushed the gate aside and rushed towards her with compassionate arms.

'Mrs Paxton! I've come about Aspen. I'm Filbert Didge. I sent you a message.'

'What?'

'I sent Gemma with a note. About Aspen being in hospital. I'm Mr Didge.'

'Then you should have said so. Come on in. Come on. You're all right. I'll shut Ashley away. Gemma come just as 'Weightwatchers' Window' was starting. I got her to read it to me, though. It was very nice.'

'I came as soon as I could. Mrs Paxton, I'm afraid it's bad news.'

'Bound to be. Bloody Northampton prices. The Education'll have to pay. Or she'll have to sell something. I'm still paying for when she had Hayley.'

115

Inside Vincent was watching 'Guto Goch a Malwen'. Two tiny girls were fighting over a perished Space Hopper. Both had dull red cheeks and glistening top lips. Didge tried not to look at them too much. It was very easy to encourage small children.

'Are they twins?'

'No. They could be. They was born the same week. I had Jade and then Aspen had Hayley. Funny really.'

'I suppose they're company for each other?'

'Yes. They fight all the time. All the time. I hardly know I've got them. How's my Aspen?'

'That's why I'm here, Mrs Paxton. I'm afraid there's very bad news. I have to prepare you for a great blow.'

'Yes?'

'I can't wrap it up. There's no way to do it except tell you, straight to the point. Aspen has died. There was nothing anyone could do. It was the middle of the night and they had to have a bank authorisation for rental of a kidney machine. I'm terribly sorry.'

'Dead?'

'I'm so sorry. I can hardly believe it myself.'

'What did she die of? Hayley, pick your feet up.'

'Shock. I think it was shock. She didn't suffer. There was no pain. She just sort of . . . fell asleep.'

'Gemma said they couldn't get him off her.'

'It did take a while.'

'Gemma said he was a Big Noise.'

'It was Clive Gribbins. An MP. He was a Minister once. Minister for Drought and Black Ice, or something like that.'

'Not Labour?'

'No, no.'

'Well there's that to be thankful for. Aspen always said she was going to make something of her life. Minister of what?'

'Just a Junior Minister. A former Junior Minister.'

'The bastard. I shall get compensation.'

'You might.'

116

'I think it's marvellous. Marvellous. We never had chances like that when we was at school.'

'I'm sorry?'

'Chances like that. We never had them. Rubbing shoulders with Big Noises. Doing it with people that's been on the telly. Will it be on the certificate?'

'What?'

'Cause of death. Will it say his name and what he done? On the certificate?'

'I don't think so. I think they limit themselves to the medical facts.'

'That's a shame. That'd have been nice to keep for Hayley.'

One of the toddlers came over.

'You going to be a good girl for your Nanna now your Mammy's gone?'

The child looked dully at Didge and wiped its nose on the arm of the sofa.

'Mammy's gone bye-byes. Hayley stop here with Nanna and Uncle Vincent.'

'Mammy gone bye-byes.'

'That's right, pet. Mammy screwed a very important man. Like a king. Jade, give them telly buttons back to Vin.'

'I shall have to be going, Mrs Paxton. Is there anything I can do? Anyone you'd like me to call? Can I fetch a neighbour to come and sit with you?'

'You got any drink on you?'

'Drink? Can I make you a cup of tea? Some strong, sweet tea might be a good idea.'

'No. A drink. Pernod. Drambuie.'

'I don't have anything like that. I'm on my way to school you see. Are there any arrangements you'd like me to see to? You won't feel up to it.'

'I shall let the Education do all that.'

'I'm sure Miss Strutt and Mr Cherish will be along to see you.'

117

'Are they from the Education? I shall take them to the cleaners.'

'Please get in touch with me if you think of anything. Anything at all.'

'And what's your name?'

'Didge. Just phone the school and ask for Mr Didge.'

'Was you the driver then?'

'I was Aspen's teacher.'

'Stop that growling, Ashley.'

'So if you're sure there's nothing I can do at the moment, I'll be off. I was very fond of Aspen. I'm really very sorry . . .'

'Well, thank you for taking her to such lovely places. I think it's marvellous.'

Hayley clung to his trouser-leg and looked up a very long way into his eyes.

'Goodbye then, little one. Goodbye.'

'Mammy gone bye-byes. Mammy crewed a very king.'

He chewed hard and kept his tears for a private moment. When he had closed the gate behind him a shoe hit him on the wrist.

'I shouldn't mind a snap.'

'A what?'

'A picture. Of the Big Wig. For Hayley.'

'I'll see what I can do. I expect they'll want things kept quiet though. In case they ever want him back in the Cabinet.'

And all the way in he rode reckless and wet-eyed, ignoring lane markings, flouting red lights, and very nearly colliding with a woman in a white coat and a silly cowboy hat as she dawdled on a zebra crossing.

Chapter 19

He hurried to be the first to tell Rosalind, but she had already been told a dozen different versions and she hadn't listened to any of them. There were other things on her mind. While Didge had been consorting with men of power, a giant wave of calamity had begun to gather, far out to sea, and now it was ready to break, carrying off everything at Freshfields that stood in its way. She ran to meet him.

'Filbert! Oh, Filbert! Something terrible!'

She flung her arms round his neck and sobbed into his woolly.

'Oh, Filbert, such a dreadful thing has happened.'

'Rosalind? Have you heard already?'

'I needed you here yesterday, Filbert. You swanned off to Northampton, and I needed you here. Headmaster has been sent away. They came yesterday and took him away.'

'Rosalind! One of my girls has died in St George's. She was set upon by an MP. And now she's dead.'

'If you say so. But Mr Cherish has been plucked from us. Our own dear Headmaster. And there's a new man already. It's all been done with indecent haste. And it gets worse, Filbert. The new man came so suddenly. I had no time to think. He came in and found me wearing that silly trouser-suit. Why did I do it? Whatever possessed me?'

'It wasn't that silly. In fact it was quite jolly. You should have come with us. I really needed you. This dreadful thing would never have happened if you'd been there.'

'He said I was improperly dressed. And I was. I haven't slept a wink, I feel so ashamed. I think things will be changing, Filbert, now Ainslie Flogger-Trimm is our man.'

The name of Flogger-Trimm staunched his grief for Aspen instantly, and replaced it with flatulent fear. Ainslie Flogger-Trimm was a cautionary tale in his own lifetime. He had started his career when morons were a minority group, and with typical far-sightedness he had made them his speciality. Morons were now the staple of every teacher's diet, and Flogger-Trimm was the expert. Hero. Bogeyman.

'Not Flogger-Trimm!'

'Oh, Filbert! It's too awful! Do you think he'll have me taken away? I've burned the trouser-suit.'

Didge felt near to death. Unauthorised expenditure. Mislaid pupils. County auditors. They all passed before him.

'Has he actually taken over? Did they say that? They might have just sent him to unsettle people. Then appoint a replacement, when things have been decided. Maybe Headmaster will come back when he's had a break.'

'But he's here, Filbert. He's been here since eight. We all have to see him in Staff Refuge at nine. Mr Boyle and Mr Nutts have to lock the girls into Big Hall while he sees us.'

There was an early morning fug in Staff Refuge. Amble and Dilly were pretending to meditate but Didge saw through all that.

Flogger-Trimm was punctual. He had the virtuous bearing of a man who had been beaten by his father and was glad of it. Everyone stood up.

'Don't sit down. I am Flogger-Trimm and you are all the scum of the earth. My duty is to do the best I can with you. Your duty will be to do exactly as you're told. The inmates of this cesspit are to be divided into three groups. The criterion will be evidence of brain activity. The categories are Dead, Departure Imminent, and Viable. The third group must not be oversubscribed. The first two groups will be interned in accordance with our statutory obligations until 00.01 hours on the day of their nineteenth birthday. To the Viable category

120

you will apply a vigorous regime of forced learning and corporal punishment. Under no circumstances may Departure Imminents be transferred to Viable. There will be a core curriculum of basic literacy and numeracy because it is required under European law. Regrettably. They will also learn simple home economy, mothercraft and marching. Any questions?'

Amble nudged Dilly and Dilly nudged him back, but it was their junior, Miss Pashley, who found the courage to ask. 'Pam Pashley, Liberal Studies. I presume we'll carry on as usual? We aim to introduce the girls to the issues of the day that are relevant to their lives. We try to take the grind out of learning and offer them a diet of what is relevant.'

'Relevant? There will be no more relevance in this establishment. It is a word I wish never to hear again. Putting the grind back into learning, that's what we're here for. It is our express purpose. Hands up all Liberal Studies skivers.'

Amble and Dilly owned up, and Didge wondered whether he counted. Out in the Annexe he didn't really belong to their set-up. None of them had ever been across to see him. Nor invited him to their end of term Wine and Cheese. He kept his hand down.

'Three? Three! Well no matter. That will free three of you immediately for sorting. After that we shall have to see. You,' he pointed to Amble, 'any good at marching?'

'Well, I don't know that I ever have.'

'Absolutely. March up and down now, by the left, one two, one two, one two.'

Amble did it very well.

'Not bad. Could be better. Take a transfer to marching.'

'I have to say, Ainslie, that I fail to see the relevance of marching.'

'Sir. That's what you will all call me. Sir. Sir is here to lift the scales from your eyes. True education asks the child to understand things that have no bearing on her life. That's the point.'

'But with respect . . .'

121

'So if we must educate these female persons let us tell them to stand back and consider something for which they cannot see any relevance.'

While Dilly and Amble strained to see the relevance of all this, Rosalind, in a selfish attempt to redeem herself over the trouser-suit, prepared to drop Didge in it. Neck deep.

'Sir, sir! Mr Didge will find himself in a difficult position. He was sent to the Annexe precisely so that he could be relevant. He's undertaken many unusual activities with his Big Girls. And outings. He's celebrated for his outings.'

'Outings? What are outings?'

'Getting out and about. Seeing for themselves what's going on in the world. Meeting real people.'

'Let Dredge speak for himself. Dredge, show yourself.'

Didge raised his hand.

'Who gave permission for jaunts? Explain.'

Didge tried for a confident tone.

'Mr Cherish of course. He was very much for them. We were at Conservative Party Local HQ yesterday. Broadening their experience.'

'Local Tory HQ? Can they put a decent crease in a pair of trousers? Can they cook a sausage without it splitting? Can they march? That's what I want to know.'

'They're coming on quite nicely.'

'You may vacate the Annexe by noon today. Deliver your charges into the custody of Mr Boyle and Mr Nutts, and vacate the premises.'

And back came Rosalind for more.

'Sir? Could you clarify what Mr Didge is to do while the Big Girls are being sorted?'

'He can report to me for paperwork.'

'Oh but I could do that for you.'

'You may bring me a glass of hot water and lemon at two. That's what you may do.'

He slammed the door behind him and the cringing snivellers

122

all waited for Wendy Wimble to check that he had gone before they began to mutter about what he had coming to him.

There were emotional scenes at the Annexe. Didge sat them down to tell them that school life would never be the same again. But they already knew. They might not know a parallelogram from a tin of peas, but they knew about Ainslie Flogger-Trimm.

Didge had grown up with the Black Man. If he came home from country dancing with odd pumps, or dropped beetroot on a clean tablecloth, he knew the Black Man would be after him. Mother had sworn it. And though his fear had never kept him from sleep for a whole night, he did still wonder and he always locked his wardrobe door last thing before he got into bed. But this was a different generation. They had grown up with cuddly extra-terrestrials and darkly evil pyjama-cases. They took the view that only the unknowable need be feared. And Flogger-Trimm had had his picture in the papers and his voice on Radio Northampton. As soon as they had heard, they knew it was all over for Didge. They tried to soften it for him.

'Never mind, Didge. We'll still come and see you.'

'Why don't you leg it while you can? We'll lend you the money.'

'Thank you, girls, thank you. You're very kind. My own future is secure for the time being. I shall be involved in administration until plans are finalised. I shall be fine. I'm more concerned with what will become of all of you.'

'We'll be all right, Didge. We've only got till Easter.'

'They won't make me go with the brainy ones will they, Didge?'

'I don't think so, Gemma.'

'I don't want to catch brains.'

'No, dear. Thank you for taking the note to Mrs Paxton.'

'I told her Aspen'd never survive it. She was watching "Weightwatchers" though.'

'And do you feel very upset by what happened to Aspen?'

'I don't know really. What's happened to Cherish?'

'Scabby Shergold said they kneecapped him.'

'No they never. He run off.'

'I heard that. He's run off.'

'He never. They put him in one of them waistcoats with no armholes. And they had to knock him out. Like this.' Lindy butted her head against the wall and stunned herself.

'Quiet, quiet. Mr Cherish is simply taking a little holiday before he reviews his career plans. He's quite well. Quite unharmed. And you must stop making up silly stories. Now listen. We have to be out of here by lunchtime. You have to gather up everything you want to take with you. Everything. Anything you leave behind may get cleared away.'

He reflected that without setting foot in the place Flogger-Trimm had succeeded where he had failed. Gemma was taking down the Christmas tree. He sat in his chair wondering what he could carry home in his saddlebag. And whether Dimity liked gadgets. And why there was a hand with silver rings touching the inside of his left thigh.

He had a look. The hand was attached to something perfumed and white. He made himself look again. It was a woman. Looking straight at him from under the brim of her stetson. Fifty, and built without a trace of simper.

'Moving house is a bad business isn't it? I'm Honeysuckle Rae Hoxie. How do you do.' And without releasing his leg she gave him her other hand and the girls looked on.

'Filbert Didge. How do you do.'

'You have some fine young women here, Filbert.'

'I do?'

'I've come to help out. To thin the numbers a little. Bella said it had better be today.'

'Of course. Bella.'

'Now, darling, she did explain I can't take them all? I have to be very particular.'

124

'Yes.'

'I'll take any that are suitable.'

'What do you want them for?'

'Straight business, angel. Only straight business. If any of them want more variety, if any of them really want to work with animals, I can put them in touch with someone.'

'Really? We have difficulty placing any of them in work. Girls, would any of you like to work with horses? Or in a cattery?'

None of them did. Honeysuckle took over.

'It's strictly straight business, girls. And I'm not a slave-driver. You'll find the working conditions second to none. France is a very civilised place.'

'France! Good heavens, girls! The chance to travel. Learn languages. See the Bayeux Tapestry. Drink wine. Will they all be together? All working together?'

'Living together. Between jobs. We don't do much group work.'

'Living together! And in France! Girls, this really is a wonderful opportunity.'

'Now let me have a good look at you, girls. I can't take any really horrid ones.'

Didge had known most of them since they were twelve. He supposed they were an ordinary bunch. Jacqui and Cindy still had their own teeth. And Mia's septic lip had cleared up nicely since she'd stopped wearing that third stud. Honeysuckle worked through them quickly. She looked into their mouths and up their skirts, and rejected out of hand all those that chewed their nails or answered her questions too smartly. A pattern began to develop. She liked them silent and sturdy. The work must call for phlegm and stamina. Pockmarks didn't matter. She took Jasmine without hesitation. And lack of hair was no bar. She accepted Lindy without waiting for her to regain consciousness.

It was getting on for twelve.

125

She said she'd take eight of them and that they should be at the Midland Station with an overnight bag at five o'clock sharp. They should finish their last day at school as if it were an ordinary day, so as not to arouse suspicions. And then she said,

'Now, Filbert, the usual terms?'

'Terms?'

'The usual. Quarterly commission. Sent through Bella. She'll act as your agent.'

'You mean I get paid?'

'Of course you do.'

'That doesn't seem right.'

'It's called business.'

'It still doesn't seem right.'

'There's nothing wrong with money, Filbert.'

'Well if you're sure?'

'I am.'

'You don't have any vacancies for men of my age?'

'No.'

'You don't know of any vacancies? I couldn't work with horses, but I'm very good with cats.'

'Sorry, dear. This is girls only. And now I'm going while the going is good. The net, sweetheart, is closing.'

She kissed him on both cheeks without disturbing her hat and left. He saw her white sleeve and her silver rings raised briefly towards Dimity's window, and she was gone.

And then the girls. He watched them go, some with bundles, some empty-handed, and Gemma with the Christmas tree. And some of them lingered, hanging on to his arm and thinking of things to ask him.

'Didge, are you taking the Soda Stream with you?'

'Didge, we've still never been to the Cheddar Gorge.'

'Can we still go to London? Can we?'

'Did you see Strutty in them trousers yesterday?'

'Do I have to go, Didge? I've got guts ache.'

126

'Girls, girls! You must all go. You know that. I'm sorry about the Cheddar Gorge. And London. I really am. Perhaps we could go on a Saturday. I don't know. But you must go to Main School.'

He put what he could into carrier bags and walked them over to Staff Refuge buffeted by the wind. He never looked back. If he had, he would have seen a dozen men in flak-jackets crawling on their bellies towards the Annexe, closing the circle.

Chapter 20

The sign that said '*Headmaster*' had been taken down already. A temporary notice said simply '*HQ – Knock*'.

He presented himself. 'It's me, sir.'

Flogger-Trimm was standing behind Cherish's desk. It had been cleared. The photograph of Mrs Cherish and her sister, the spider-plant with the brown leaves, the little brass bell with the stag's head handle that was 'A Present from Tomintoul'. All gone. All wrapped in brown paper and labelled Psychiatric Assessment Unit, Leicester Forest East. In their place were papers. Letters, circulars, memos, accounts rendered. Didge felt uneasy.

'You are going to help me.'

'Yes, sir?'

'Yes, Dodgy. You're just the man for the job.'

'Yes, sir?'

'You can go through the accounts with me. Together we shall persuade these pieces of paper to give up their terrible secrets. And when we have, Dodgy, heads will roll.'

'Yes, sir.'

'Explain to me the following items. An invoice from Wet Dreams Ltd of Wellingborough for the design and installation of a circular three-speed jacuzzi in a place called the Annexe.'

'Sir?'

'And from Stenstrom Body Beauty Inc. for the supply of one Aphrodite Solarium with goggles and instruction booklet, one mains-operated Faradic Massager, and one Contour De-Luxe Facial Sauna. All Balls Sports Equipment of Market Harborough for one seven foot snooker table with foldaway leg-units

128

and a maple-shafted cue with hardwood butt and canvas carrying case.'

Didge felt as though he was fitted with foldaway leg-units. And Flogger-Trimm was still getting up speed.

'Bliss and Buck Bathrooms and Kitchens for the supply of one Osawa Mark Six Microwave Cooker, one Atlantic City Waffle-Maker and a Nippy Two-Litre Deep-Fryer with locking filter lid.'

He decided to speak up before the food-processor and the tumble-dryer were mentioned.

'It was Mr Cherish, sir.'

'Yes?'

'Yes. He was a very eccentric man. He thought we needed things in the Annexe. He was very eccentric. And very insistent.'

He shifted feet and thought about the bags he'd left in Staff Refuge. At least the air-purifier was his own by right.

'Mr Cherish?'

'Yes.'

'He authorised all of this?'

'Oh yes, sir. He was doing it all the time. We were all concerned about it, but he was at the helm so to speak. And he was a much loved man.'

'Loved?'

'Oh yes.'

'What about a potato-peeler with salad-spinner and juice-extractor attachments? Or a laser-powered freezer knife?'

'I'm sure he intended to pay for them, sir.'

'A one-hundred-and-twenty-five-litre electric concrete-mixer?'

'Hard to say, sir.'

'A ZIT portable arc-welder?'

'I know he hoped to re-open the Metalwork Department. In the fullness of time.'

'Dregs, you are named in many of these invoices. Your name is clearly typed for all to see.'

129

Didge's stomach, neglected since the sandwiches on Kev's Vista Coach, began to cut loose, and the floor tilted at an inconsiderate angle. He was a hopeful man but not stupid. He had known this day would come. But he had expected to deal with the vague and compliant Cherish. He had not planned on Flogger-Trimm.

There were five or six explosions in rapid succession. The ground floor of the Annexe was hidden by black smoke in seconds and he could see men sitting on the ridge of the roof.

'My God! It's the Annexe! It's burning!'

'It's being tidied up.'

'But all the equipment . . .'

'Nothing worth keeping.'

'. . . and Mrs Hubble. Mrs Hubble is still up there.'

'Nothing worth keeping.'

'But she's going to get hurt!'

'What have you done with the laser-powered freezer knife, Diggs?'

'But you mustn't hurt her. She isn't doing any harm up there. She doesn't stand a chance.'

A single bigger explosion ripped through the inside of the Annexe. The smoke came in bursts, covering everything, and then the wind moved it on, allowing Didge to see.

Men were advancing on the house under cover of riot shields, and, travelling across the mud of the old hockey-field, there were two demolition vehicles under heavy woodland camouflage. One of the rooftop squad began to abseil down the side of the building. As his feet reached the sill of an upstairs window he prepared to toss in a canister of tear-gas. But, before he could do it, he took an almighty blow below the belt and was sent boomeranging along the wall, until he was knocked senseless and hung there, as limp as a jack in the doldrums. Somewhere someone cheered. Then an improvised rope began to appear through the charred window frame. A dress length of corded poplin had been knotted to a roll-end of crêpe de Chine viscose, and down it, in a terracotta flying-suit with stud fastenings and an unusual trim of inset faggoting, slid Dimity Hubble.

As her feet touched the ground, two khaki gorillas tried to floor her, but she was ready for them. The pinking shears were all she had been able to carry away, and they stood her in good stead. She had the gorillas licked.

Overcome with bravado, Didge opened Flogger-Trimm's window without even asking if he could, and followed her progress. She scarpered across the front lawn and, as she cleared the Staniforth Memorial Rose Bed, a powerful motorbike roared into the car park. Leathered like a despatch rider, Dimity's rescuer kept the revs high, and, as she swung her leg over the pillion, gave the throttle so much boot that they were out of the gates and gone before she had had time to clip on her crash-hat.

The Rubble Riders never stopped. Before Didge left for an indefinite period of unpaid leave, the front of the Annexe was completely out and the back wall was crumbling.

And on the other side of the school the climbing frames were being dismantled, to make all the more room for marching.

Hedley was glad to see him. He brought him a cup standing in a saucer of strong tea and showed him the pictures he'd been cutting out of Our Royal Family. Daddo was in his chair with a rolled towel in his lap.

'You're home early.'

'Bit of a shake up at school. What's the matter with you?'

'Strained me groin. You got the sack?'

'I'm taking some leave.'

'He's got the sack.'

'How have you strained your groin?'

'It's me age.'

'You were making a lot of noise last night. You probably banged yourself against the edge of the bed.'

'That's it, son.'

'What's in the towel?'

'Ice cubes.'

'That's the thing to do is it? Ice cubes?'

'Oh yes. Just the job. You seem a bit down, son. Gave you the push have they?'

'No, I told you. I'm taking some leave. Colin Cherish is taking a sabbatical and they're restructuring things. It'll give me time to catch up on some reading. Time to think.'

'You have all them long holidays for that. No wonder this country's gone down the nick.'

'People who haven't been teachers never understand. The pressures are enormous. Books to be marked, teaching standards under constant scrutiny, the pastoral care of all those young lives. It takes its toll. Batteries have to be recharged.'

'So you'll be stopping at home will you, son?'

Hedley greeted this proposition with touching pleasure. He topped up Didge's tea and set about a picture of Princess Victoria with his tongue stuck out and his scissors moving carefully.

'I shall have things to do of course. Letters to write. People to visit. I shall have plenty to do.'

His ManPower uniform hung ready for the evening. Glenda had gone over it with the Dabitoff.

'You could go away, son. Have a proper little holiday.'

'And leave you two?'

'Glenda could keep an eye on us.'

'No.'

'I was only thinking of you, son. We shall get on each other's nerves, else. You know what you're like. And we don't want you under our feet neither. Do we, boy?'

Loyally Hed refused to stop smiling at him.

'I shan't get under your feet. I shall be busy.'

'When will you be going back, son?'

'We've left it open. There was no hurry to fix a date.'

'Have they gave you your P88?'

'No. I'm tired of explaining it.'

'Well you don't want to leave it like that. If you don't have it definite that you're going back, anything could happen. Have you been in trouble? Is it her with no eyelashes?'

'What?'

'I thought so. I thought you were well in there at Christmas. Caught at it were you?'

'What are you talking about?'

'Nookie.'

'Did you have anything special planned for tea? Or shall we just let Cook surprise us as usual?'

While the chip fat got hot he made a list of all the things he had had to leave at school and drew a thick line right through it. Then he ate his chips like a free man.

Things were getting a bit out of hand at ManPower. He enjoyed the talks and was managing the squat-thrusts better than before. And he loved the songs at the end. He was prepared to agree that he did enjoy the sing-songs. But the linking hands and the pledging were getting very fervent. He didn't care for a lot of bodily contact himself. And sometimes their hands got wet with emotion.

If there had been someone there, to be pledged to, it wouldn't have seemed quite so daft. But it was such a vague arrangement. They didn't have his name or address, nor any idea of when he might be expected. They were just certain that He would show up one of these days, and that they'd know Him. By The Mark.

At the beginning he'd gone along with it. It was something to look forward to – like a new bike if you passed for the Grammar. And he had looked at men, discreetly. As they

133

checked their oil and bought Gro-Bags for their marrows and did the things men do, he'd searched them for The Mark. And they'd all had something. Warts. Freckles. The scars of old Home Improvement battles.

He was glad Corrigan was so clued up about it all. If it came Corrigan's way, it wouldn't go unnoticed. He'd end the suspense one of those days.

For himself Didge had had enough. He'd met some nice people and learned a lot about wimmin. He had gained the self-assurance that comes from knowing the enemy well, and he'd gone back to wearing one pair of underpants. But he didn't want to be tied any more. He had decided to stick it out until Spring Manoeuvres. Have his weekend in Wales, now bought and paid for, and then make his excuses.

As it was a warm evening and fresh air made for a purer night's sleep, they did their exercises on the grass in front of the Scout Hut. Didge hated it. Wimmin came by and made him get out of step. And then men, sinister with haircuts and Bibles, who smiled over the privet and said,

'Are you ready for Him when He comes?'

They missed out working in pairs on the Inner Leg Hook and the Front Snap Kick and went inside. Corrigan said they should avoid contact with these wandering lunatic elements and that it was time to check their kit list for Spring Camp.

Didge knew it by heart. And he knew he had everything, ready and named. Sleeping-bag, mess-can, torch and batteries, thick woollen socks, waterproof cape, something to do in case it was wet. He had it all ready except the cape. And he knew that he had that somewhere. Put away safely.

Boyle said he'd booked the coach and his brother to drive it. Nutts said the cocoa was ordered. And Corrigan showed them slides of where they would be going. It was a good place for men, he explained. Something had got into the water and the wimmin had all gone haywire. Hiked off to Polytechnics and

134

Peace Camps. Bankrupted the hairdressers and the wool-shop. It was a place for men now. Where they could walk safely, claim their own space, and furthermore it was lovely walking country.

So they pledged themselves to dubbin their boots and know Him when He came, and Didge biked home to have another look for that waterproof.

Chapter 21

He left the house every morning, as though he still had a job. He watched from the edge of the playing-field, through the sudden spiteful showers, and the sun that followed them and hurt his eyes, and gathered what he could of the new regime. Every day started the same. Two brisk circuits of the old hockey-pitch and then a cold hosing down by the Staff Entrance. Then, just before the girls arrived, they were allowed to change back into their working clothes.

Mia brought him sausage-rolls and said he should go home before he was noticed or caught a cold. She came every day. Once she brought a postcard from Lindy and the others who now called Honeysuckle 'Momma'. It said they were happy and doing a lot of meeting people.

But mostly she brought grim news. There were no more projects. No discussion groups or field studies. Instead there were hours of learning by rote. And marching. Miles of it. Plain marching for the juniors. Marching with a supermarket trolley for the seniors. And there was drilling. How to Strip and Clean a Room. Basic Rules of Stain Removal. The Clearing of Gutters and Downpipes. According to Mia a coat of zinc chromate primer was not to be sneered at.

He did catch a cold but it didn't keep him at home. Flogger-Trimm had added Talking to Men to the curriculum and had promised to drill the seniors personally, out on the field where there was no scope for drowsiness or unwholesomeness. Didge eavesdropped as Flogger-Trimm gave them the lead and they recited after him, 'Good evening, my dearest, your supper is ready and waiting. Your slippers are warming by the hearth.

Your racing paper is ironed and awaiting your pleasure. That is no job for a man, no, no, I insist. Is there anything further you require of me, or may I replace the sponge head on my mop?' They all knew what to say. They were word perfect.

He felt a weight lift from him. His girls would be all right. It was nearly Easter and they were doing fine.

He missed a couple of days after that and, when he came back, he had lost his place. Where he had flattened the grass and kept a concerned eye on things, a mountain of potatoes had been dumped. Wendy Wimble and Pam Pashley were loading them into buckets, and the senior girls were waiting, blunted knives at the ready, to learn a new and useful skill.

Didge stayed very still, lest the shock of seeing him crouched there should unhinge them into ravishing his body, and, when they'd filled the buckets and gone, he righted his bike and turned away from the place for the last time.

He wanted to have one more go at finding his waterproof. That was the trouble with the cubby-hole. It was a handy place to put things, on your way in, on your way out. But, once they were in there, things drifted and settled, and somehow old newspapers were the only thing that ever came to the surface. So many things of value and usefulness had come to grief in there. Duffle-coats that were nearly the right size for someone. Handy inspection lamps that went under and wouldn't come up for air until their batteries had leaked. And perished hot-water bottles that might come in for something. When he was a little boy, a spare mangle had been committed to that cubby-hole, and to his certain knowledge it had never been seen again.

And now it had eaten his waterproof when he really did need it for Wales.

He started, calmly and systematically, putting all the old newspapers in one pile, and all the things that were too good to be thrown away in another. But gradually his temper got the

137

better of him, and when Daddo came down, wearing only his Harley Davidson sweatshirt, to see about the noise, he had just found the pram. It had a sprung chassis and a shopping-tray so he asked Daddo what the hell it was doing there. And Daddo said it had been a special offer in one of Hedley's catalogues and how it was sure to be useful one fine day. How it was sure to come in.

'Come in?'

'Handy.'

'Handy?'

'For moving things about.'

'What things?'

'Bags of compost. Calor gas cylinders.'

'But it's brand new.'

'It's got a two-wheel brake and a secondary locking device. It was a very good price. For what you were getting.'

They lifted the pram back in and Daddo told him how Tufnell might have borrowed the waterproof. They parted friends, Daddo back up to his bed, and Didge to Wales, with the promise of a lend of the pram any time he had need of it.

Dinas Mawddwy was ready for Spring Manoeuvres. The rain had fallen steadily through the month of March and Costas the Chip had strung the fish-shop front with coloured lights and upped his prices by half.

Everyone else had been the year before and knew the ropes. Tents were pitched, provisions were stowed, weapons were drawn, and no one bothered with him, so he went for several exploratory crouches until he worked out that for the longer functions the only safe course was to take his trousers off altogether and hold them well out of the way. And that it was best not to be hasty. And not to cut corners on the toilet paper, just because he was camping.

Even the cocoa failed to soothe him. He was so excited about waking up under canvas that he lay awake all night

138

listening to the wetness outside and wondering if he could hold on with his legs crossed till daylight.

Corrigan showed them on a map how the coach would take them to Bala and wait while they walked round the lake. All the way round. Didge wished his boots were as comfortable as Bellingham's. Somewhere on the way they saw a woman. The rougher types banged on the windows and jeered at her. It was the side of things he didn't care for at all. But then Boyle started them singing 'I Love To Go A-wandering' and he joined in and let the moment of sourness pass.

It was not to be a good day. Glenda's socks chafed though she'd promised him faithfully they wouldn't, and the weather was Welsh and evil. When it rained, it rained, which was fair enough. But when the sun came out he got up too much steam inside his nylon jacket, and, if he took it off, the wind drove him into perished misery. And there were flies. At a time of year when all flies should decently be dead. He wished he'd learned how to smoke cigarettes. And how to tie a nylon cagoule round his middle.

When they got back to Dinas, and Robbo and Lewis had tucker ready, they fell on the Boil-in-a-Sack Bacon and Beans and bickered when the Wagon Wheels didn't quite go round. After all, they were men, ravenous from a day in the wild, raw from surviving by their wits. Before they could face an evening of homespun entertainment they needed to be properly fed. They slipped away in twos and threes, staggering their times, so that their numbers never looked too thin. Didge went with Nipley and Bellingham, despite the soreness of his feet, and, as he came to the head of the queue, tantalised by the smell of hot vinegar, he panicked and over-ordered.

Nipley got quite narked about having to wait for him while he finished the third meat pie. In the end he dropped the last of the mushy peas over someone's chain-link fence and they

139

hurried back to camp, waving their arms to get rid of the smell.

Rising Free. That was what Corrigan had called the evening. It was to express the growing energy of ManPower, and everyone had to do something. Nipley was going to sing. Bellingham was going to conjure with string. Didge had said he would play for them on comb and tissue paper which was a beastly lie. He had actually worked out that he could time an urgent call of nature just before he was called on. And failing that he would show them the Gay Gordons. All on his own. Without music. But it never came to it.

When Rickard had finished whistling 'In A Monastery Garden', Boyle warned Didge he was on after the next turn. This gave him time for an authentic display. He held his belly and rocked. He alluded to the risks of reheated meat pies. And he apologised to his nearest neighbours for any offence caused. Then, as Pratley Junior went into the second verse of 'Rouse the Gut with Drum and Trumpet', he got up and bolted into the dripping rhododendrons.

It was just an ordinary mark. White. Shiny. Just a scar. It had knitted over the memory of being made to go blackberrying with Mother. She had insisted on it. It had been all very well for Hedley. He'd never had to go. He'd never had to go anywhere. The cunning little toad had learned that if he hid his balaclava he'd get left behind. Mother wasn't having anyone see him without his balaclava. And if the day was too hot for a balaclava, even for someone with ears like Hedley's, he'd wet himself and be left behind as punishment. It never failed.

So every year Didge had had to go with her. Every year a little earlier than the last so as to steal a march on everyone else and gather them by the pound. Too many to eat straight off. Pans full of them that had to be made into jam. Had to be. It was such a saving. And though Mother was a woman of many talents, jam-making had not been one of them.

140

She saw other pickers as interlopers. Plunderers of the countryside. She vied with them so fiercely that she'd pick anything sooner than leave it for another day. She picked them red. She picked them green. She even picked the ones at dog-leg height. And they all went into the jam.

And that was how he had come by his mark. Mother had spotted a ripe cluster just beyond her reach and wouldn't go home till it was hers. She had tried standing on the broken deckchair someone had left in the ditch. She had tried standing on him. Neither of them would bear her weight. So she had lifted him, egging him on for just one more, just that big one, until he had lost his balance and had fallen, tearing himself on the barbed wire.

Soon after that he'd gone off to college and Mother had died, so the blackberrying had stopped. Daddo had given the collecting bags to Tufnell, Hedley had done a bodily function in the jam pan, and Didge had been left with his scar.

It was Nipley and Pangbourne who came upon him in that wet gloom with his trousers in his hand for authenticity. And it was Pangbourne whose voice went up first. He always was inclined towards the hysterical. The only man in Kettering who had blankets and a ludo board under his stairs in case nuclear annihilation arrived sooner than Corrigan reckoned. Now he fell to his knees and lost control.

'The Mark. The Mark. He has The Mark. He has come. He was amongst us all the time. I felt it. I always felt it. He has The Mark.'

Nipley was more cautious. He came closer and fingered the cheek of Didge's behind, running his nail over the shape of the scar while Didge stood frozen. And then he joined in:

'The Mark. The Mark . . .'

Just a few came at first. They'd heard Pangbourne and assumed he'd been caught short without toilet paper. Then Nicolson had refused to go on because there was so much

141

noise coming from the undergrowth, and his whole audience got up and left him with his squeeze-box.

That was when things really caught fire. It may have been something the shifty Cypriot had put in the battered cod. Or the effect of thirty-six hours of wet and foreign tedium. Or pre-ordained. Mapped out in the stars for anyone silly enough to read it. Whatever it was, the contagion was total. A great wailing of thankfulness and rending of garments possessed that Welsh hillside, and by eight o'clock Rising Free lay in ruins, and Didge's bottom had been touched in wonderment by thirty-seven emotional men.

Corrigan, wild-eyed, declared that they must strike camp that night. He wanted to get Didge back into places where the publicity machine could do its work, before imposters were proclaimed in places like St Neots.

The careful order with which they had unpacked the day before was lost. Tinned fruit, wet clothing, sausages, ammo. They were all stuffed willy-nilly into the luggage space. And Corrigan wouldn't let Didge do a thing for himself. He made him sit in the seat of his choice, while the coach was prepared, and wouldn't let him out of his sight, even when a fight broke out as to who should be allowed to pack for Him Who Had Come.

Corrigan asked him solicitously if he'd care for some hot Bovril, even though there was none to be had. And all Didge could say, over and over, was 'This is all very silly, Terence. Very silly. It's only a silly old fruit-picking wound.'

Chapter 22

They drove through the night. Boyle had the idea that they might drop pieces of paper with tidings of great joy, in centres of population as they passed through, but in Welshpool, as they cruised and looked for likely dropping points, there were so many wimmin about that none of them had the stomach for pamphleteering, and they drove on in the interests of Didge's health and safety.

It was three o'clock on Sunday morning when they got him home. On the M6 a three-cornered cabal had emerged. Corrigan, Boyle and Nutts. There was a certain logic behind it. They had known him intimately and long, counted themselves amongst his closest friends when he was nothing a pound, and knew he would think of them first when it came to bestowing apostolic office. Corrigan was also secretly concerned that Didge might try to flit. He had not expected He who bore The Mark to be so reluctant. So while Didge dozed it was agreed that the three of them would finish out the night at the foot of His bed like the most faithful of disciples.

Didge wouldn't hear of it. He had never shared a bedroom in his life and he wasn't starting now. He told them to go home, calm down, and see how things looked in the morning light.

When the coach stopped, too big for the road and too noisy for the hour, Glenda happened to be up and looking out. It was the time of night she usually got up to make a drink and check the front garden for vandals and wimmin. She boarded the coach in her dressing-gown and viewed the chaos. Nothing had been properly packed. Sugar and milk were spilt underfoot. Single socks had strayed. And there were men, who had thrown themselves onto the mud in glad obeisance, who would have a lot of explaining to do when they got home.

She took charge. Didge's key had gone missing, but she had a spare one. He wouldn't yield over the sleeping arrangements but she fetched blankets and pillows from her own house and arranged it all so well that Daddo and Hedley slept straight through.

As soon as there were signs of life, Corrigan went down to explain how things stood. Glenda was there already, telling Daddo that last night had been nearly as exciting as the war, and scissoring the rind off the bacon for him. Didge felt bashful about eating his breakfast with all of them watching him. He could have eaten a horse, but Corrigan kept saying things like 'I was blind not to have seen it before. Everything he does, everything he says, marks him out as . . . different', until he had to line up his knife and fork and admit defeat.

Then there were comings and goings. It was like a house where there had been a sudden death. Arrivals at the front door. People saying things that people don't say. And no one knowing or caring what the time was.

Nipley was one of the first. He bowed deeply to Didge and said Northamptonshire was aglow. After all the travelling, ManPower had set out, happy and exhausted, to tell Wellingborough and Corby that He had come, that Kettering claimed Him for its very own, and to pass it on. Corby had showed no resistance. They were glad they could stop looking, and had sent men out at first light to tell Peterborough and Market Harborough.

Wellingborough had not been so easy. Their second-in-command had been difficult about being woken so early, and had said he had a small scar on the inside of his left thigh if anyone was interested. But in the end there had come a begrudging generosity towards Kettering and Didge. Welling-

144

borough had said they would ratify him as an *ad hoc* One Who Bore The Mark, provided he addressed their rally that very evening and drove their membership to frenzied commitment. Otherwise they'd have to reconsider. Corrigan sneered.

'Typical of Wellingborough. Typical. It's sheer jealousy, of course. Wellingborough has always been a very envious place.'

'So will that be all right then? Can we tell them he'll be there?'

'Of course he'll be there. He'll give them something to think about. Leave them reeling.'

'He's looking a bit tired.'

'He'll find the strength. Those who Get the Call always do. You can do it can't you, Didge?'

'What's that?'

'Satisfy these sceptics. Create a landslide in Wellingborough.'

'Terence, this is very silly.'

'I quite agree. But it's in the best of traditions. Cast your mind back. It's never been easy for prophets. There's always been egg-throwing. Always a spot of ostracism.'

'But the whole thing is silly. We should still be in Wales. We should be doing Guerrilla Warfare and then into Barmouth for tea.'

'This is more important than Spring Manoeuvres. This is what we're really about. Leadership. It's what we've been waiting for. We'll show Wellingborough.'

'But I don't want to go to Wellingborough.'

'Oh you'll have to. You'll have to. You don't want to let people down, son.'

'I don't care about people. Not people in Wellingborough. Why should I care a damn about them?'

'All you've got to do is stand up and say a few words. Tell them to go forth and prepare themselves for victory. Tell them the hour is nigh.'

And then Glenda interfered, standing gouging the congealed

bits from behind the taps with an old knife and getting in everybody's way.

'I'll see he gets there.'

'There's no need for that. We'll get up an escort.'

'I'd go myself only Tufnell said he'd drop in later.'

'And I'd go myself but there's things to be done here. Kettering's really going to be on the map by tomorrow morning. Right in the front line.'

Didge found them irritating. He was tired of doors opening and shutting, and people falling to their knees. Rosalind just about crowned it. She came round the back way, as though she'd been calling for years, and said she wondered how things were, and did Didge know that Pam Pashley had run away with Alan Amble, and the potato mountain had gone rotten and stunk because the girls had worked too slowly and Swills, who was never slow to profit from others' misfortunes, had bought a pig to eat them, and did he know that people were taking away little bits of his front fence?

Daddo and Corrigan went out to see about that and it was true. The trafficking in relics had begun already, and men walked by, slowly, just looking. They marked that afternoon as something different. If Didge had been free to go for a wander he would have felt it, too. It was no ordinary Sunday. Back gates, bay curtains, minds, all usually closed against danger and fresh air, were left open to all risks, and habits of a lifetime were jettisoned. A man from Desborough who had had relations with his wife on an old towel on the bathroom floor every Sunday for twenty-seven years, even during the Falklands conflict, set out for Kettering without properly digesting his Yorkshire pudding and died on the side of the A6 without ever catching sight of Him Who Had Come. And in Brigstock they defied the cold and held a street party.

Rosalind stayed and stayed. She'd shaved her legs and it seemed to have gone to her brain. When he said he wouldn't go to Wellingborough because his feet were still sore, she fetched

146

a tub of Nivea out of her bag and massaged it into his blisters in front of everyone.

'Oh, Filbert! I knew you were special!'

'Rosalind!'

'But I did! The way you never fitted in. I noticed it a long time ago.'

'Rosalind, this is silly. They've got the wrong chap.'

'They haven't, Filbert. They haven't. I'm so proud to be associated with you. You're what this country needs.'

'I'm not.'

'You are. You are. You're going to make Mummy and all those rude wimmin stay off the streets and behave themselves. Restore old values.'

'I'm not.'

'You are!'

'Not!'

'Oh, Filbert! And then Ainslie will beg you to come back to school. Oh I do miss you.'

Daddo and Hedley enjoyed this. They followed the conversation backwards and forwards across the table and smiled. And then they stitched him up. It was agreed that while they fended off cranks and journalists, Corrigan would organise a massive turnout to welcome him back from Wellingborough, Nipley would escort him to the rally, Rosalind would drive him because she had a car and wouldn't shut up till they let her do something, and Glenda would cut the sandwiches.

By teatime there was nothing left of the front gate, and on their way out they frightened off a man with a penknife who was after a bit of the window frame.

They made Didge sit in the back under a blanket. Nipley sat in the front with Rosalind, and they kept it up all the way to Wellingborough.

'I can't wait to hear you speak, Filbert!'

'You won't be let in. Wimmin aren't allowed.'

'But I'm his driver.'

'You still won't be let in.'

'I think he'll make a very inspiring speaker. I think he'll bring them to their feet.'

'He'll need to. They're hard men in Wellingborough.'

'What are you going to say to them, Filbert?'

'Nothing.'

'Filbert!'

'I don't want to go there. The place has nothing to recommend it and I'm suffering from mistaken identity.'

'You'll have to speak to them. That's what they'll have come for. To hear a message.'

'Well, you speak to them then.'

'Now you're being ridiculous.'

'I don't know what to say. You speak to them.'

'Just say inspirational things. Tell them you're a simple humble man. Who won't shirk his duty no matter how painful.'

'That's good. I like that. Then he could tell them that the road will be long . . .'

'And hard.'

'Yes. And then he could tell them to go forth.'

'Oh yes! That's a must!'

Didge saw his name sprayed on the boarded windows of the old Co-op, and heard Nipley tell Rosalind that thousands were gathering, and would he get back under his bloody blanket before he was spotted. Somehow nothing prepared him for what awaited them in Wellingborough's Cumberland Hall.

Nipley had been mistaken. There weren't thousands. There were hundreds, and that was enough. The grey of Man-Power stretched as far as his eye could see, with banners and flags and petrol-soaked effigies of wimmin. For her own safety Rosalind said she would stay in the car, and Didge was surprised to find how much he felt the lack of her. She seemed

148

to know exactly what he should do. Seemed so glad to be associated with it.

Nipley guided him to the front of the platform where Wellingborough Command sat waiting to be utterly amazed. In a moment of spontaneity Didge raised his arms to the men who had come so far to see him. He wanted to ask them for mercy and forbearance but, before he had said a word, they answered him with a roar of voices and a flash of brass on ribbons, and then with a dreadful silence.

Nipley prompted him from the right, *sotto voce*, 'I am a simple and humble man . . .' And, if only he could have heard her, Rosalind was out there at the back mouthing the same words and wondering which of the warrior men would have his way with her if she were noticed. She couldn't have stayed away. You could smell the excitement from the car park.

He began, 'I'm a simple, humble man. No one is more surprised than me to find myself here tonight.'

'Tell them you won't shirk the burden laid upon you.'

'Leadership is not a thing that has ever appealed to me. I'm a backroom boy. Always have been. And as much as I think there is work to be done, things that need putting right, I know you'd do a lot better with someone like our own Corrigan. A born leader if ever I saw one.'

This was not at all what Nipley wanted.

Those in the middle, who hadn't heard too well, reported to those at the back, who hadn't heard at all, that he was a man who had found himself and that under him everything would be well to the Right. But those at the front were swaying and hissing dissatisfaction.

'For my own part, I'd rather find the middle road. Don't get me wrong. I know wimmin have to be kept in hand. We all know that. But need we be so drastic? I don't think so. I think wimmin respond to a little kindness. Doors held open. Flowers. Chocolates . . .'

149

Nipley was in the terminal stages of despair. He beseech-
ed Didge, 'For Christ's sake tell them to go forth!' and
then, inspired, began to tug at his trousers. 'Show them the
mark.'

Those near enough to catch his words repeated them and the
ripples spread.

'The Mark! The Mark! Show us The Mark!' The whole
caucus ranted it and chanted it while Didge dodged Nipley and
Nipley tackled him for his trousers. Somewhere in the middle
two rival groups tangled. Some were for him, some were agin
him. And for the first time in her life Rosalind acted with utter
mindlessness. She raised her voice with the rest, calling, 'The
Mark! Oh, Filbert, do show us The Mark!' oblivious to the
silence that was spreading around her.

It didn't take the men of Wellingborough long to see her for
what she was, and change their cry.

'A wimmin! It's one of them wimmin! Get her!'

As Didge held tight to his belt and tried to duck off the side
of the platform, Rosalind went down under a heap of warrior
men. She went down so easily she threw them off balance, and,
having got her to the floor, those that were closest to her didn't
know what they ought to do next. They just sat on her and
mulled it over.

Two of Wellingborough's grosser specimens tried to block
Didge's way but he distracted them with a Two-Fingered
Eyeball Poke, and stumbled through the warren of passages
that ran behind the stage, setting off every fire alarm he passed
on his way to freedom. There were no more challenges. Inside
they had turned their attentions to Nipley. Hundreds of them
had removed their trousers to taunt him with their unmarked
behinds, and under it all, a reedy and excited voice still begged,
'Come on, Filbert. Take your trousers off. There's no call to be
shy.'

Outside he was ignored. He was just another man in grey,
and the crowds there were too intent on getting in to see the

150

thing that had come to pass, to bother with a total stranger. Nothing stood between him and Rosalind's little car. Nothing stood between him and escape. Except Rosalind. She was the driver. And she was inside, waiting to be interfered with.

Chapter 23

He sat in the car and warmed up a little while he addressed himself to the immediate problem. He had never driven anything bigger than a bike. He had a rough idea but he had to abort a number of launches before he found first gear and leap-frogged onto the A510.

By lighting up time he was feeling very pleased with himself. Not only had he worked out the headlamps and the sidelights but he'd also found the rear fogs and decided to keep them on, just in case.

There are those who would feel impatient to progress beyond second gear, but Didge was enjoying himself. The number of people who overtook him was astonishing and every one of them took time out to wave. Motoring evidently brought out the very best in people.

Eventually, in a little burst of cockiness, he dared to turn left and tack across country to Burton Latimer. He felt invincible. He experimented with the headlamp dipper. Everyone else seemed to be flashing all over the place. Perhaps it was the thing to do?

It was only his slowing down to do a bit of dipping that allowed him to notice a figure on the roadside ahead. It was flagging him down with a white scarf. At twenty miles an hour he had time to work out whether it was the police or whether it was someone he should stop for. And at the very last moment his lights picked out Bella Strutt, zipped into her motor bike leathers and tugging at her crash helmet so that he would see her face.

In his surprise he forgot which pedal slowed the thing down, and eventually he came to a halt by taking his foot off the gas, as the road began to climb, and letting the engine stall. The car rolled back silently until Bella wrenched the passenger door open, fell in and applied the handbrake with both hands.

'Bella!'

'Thank goodness! I was beginning to think we'd missed you. You're so late. Where have you been?'

'Oh, Bella, I'm so pleased to see you. I've had a terrible time. I've done a bunk. And I've done something unforgivable. I've left Ros behind. And I know she'd be only too happy to make that bloody speech, but it's a man they want. They'll give her a bad time. And I've never played with one of these things before. They're so slow. And yet they feel so fast when other people drive them.'

'Move across into this seat. I'll just tell Dim.'

She jumped out and ran back to where another figure was waiting with the bike. They exchanged a few words and Bella returned, this time to the driver's seat. She threw the car onto the road and drove it hard into the stream of traffic.

'Belt up, Filbert.'

'Sorry?'

'Your belt. Fasten it. And tell me how you've managed in one evening what I've been trying to do for forty years.'

'Sorry?'

'Given Ros the slip.'

'I'm really sorry. I feel awful about it. How will she get home?'

'Very slowly I hope.'

'She was so determined I should go. I told her I didn't want to. But she went on and on about sense of duty. And taking a pride. She said her father would have got up there and spoken to them.'

'Yes, he would.'

'We'd better go back for her.'

'Filbert! We've only just got rid of her. She'll find her way back. Sooner than you'd think possible.'

'But they might turn on her. Or she might get lost.'

'She can read signposts.'

'What about if she falls among wimmin?'

'We can only hope.'

'How did you find me?'

'Luck. You were sighted in Finedon. Then we lost you.'

'I turned left.'

'In the end we just guessed.'

'Who was that with you?'

'Dimity. She said to say hello. She's taking the bike back to Kettering. She can travel faster than us.'

Didge found this hard to believe.

'Why did you come looking for me?'

'There's trouble ahead. Quite a reception waiting for you by now I should imagine. You're a wanted man. Wanted by men. Wanted by wimmin. Take my word for it, there'll be others wanting you before the night's out.'

'Bella, I'm so tired. I just want to give back my uniform and go to bed.'

'Out of the question. You must get away quickly. I want you on a train out of Kettering tonight. We're as ready as we're going to be. I'll take you straight home, and you're to go in over the back fence. That will give us more time at the front.'

'What's going to happen?'

'We can't be sure. I expect there'll be blood.'

'I don't know if I can get over the back fence.'

'I'll give you a leg up. When you're in you'll have to be quick. We've lost enough time as it is. Hedley has a change of clothes for you and a bag. You can take whatever you can carry in one bag, but you must be quick. When you're ready you can leave by the front door. Hedley knows the signal. And we have a little diversion planned.'

154

It took three tries to get him over the fence and he grazed his shin badly. He stumbled through the blackcurrant bushes, tangled with the washing-line and narrowly missed the cold-frame. As his hand touched the back door it opened and in the darkened kitchen he found Hedley, standing there, waiting.

Hedley had thought of everything. The kettle was on the gas and there was a bowl of cling peaches and evaporated milk saved from teatime. Even the cat had been made to stay in so that it could be said good-bye to.

Hedley had laid out the clothes on the back of the settee. Didge stripped down to his boxer shorts and Hedley gave him a pair of Extra Large panty-hose in Sombrero Tan. He laughed at the joke, and then looked more closely at the rest of the clothes. They were women's. Didge said he wouldn't, and Hed said he must. He pointed towards the front of the house and made the sign of a throat being cut.

'But where has all this come from?'

Hedley fetched his mail order catalogues and showed Didge the very pages. He helped Didge take the tights off and put them on the right way round. They bagged round his ankles and the crotch wouldn't reach, but the colour was very pleasing. When it came to it they didn't bother with the brassiere, or the padding. Didge had bosom enough as it was. They moved on to the polyester two-piece. Dusk Rose wasn't really Didge. But the fit was perfect. And with the headscarf, the mock-coney jacket and the plain but tasteful court shoes, he made a handsome sight. He just wished the shoes might have been a little bit vulgar. He slipped them off while he went upstairs to have a look in his mirror and collect what he wanted. The bag Bella had promised him was only a clutch purse. It wouldn't hold any-thing to speak of. He slipped his spare specs and his credit cards into it, with the picture of Mother and Daddo at Mablethorpe, and the Lonely Nites Velvi Gluv. There was no picture of Hedley to take. Mother had never allowed it.

He looked round the room for the last time. And then,

cautiously, out of the window. The street was packed with men. And there was a banner, but it drooped from its long wait and its message was hidden. They were still. Massed in a grim and silent vigil.

He put his hands on Hedley's shoulders and looked at him gravely.

'Be a good boy, Hed. Be a good lad for Daddo. Eh? You've done very well tonight. With the clothes. Did the lady tell you what to get? The nice lady? You did very well. Don't look like that. I shall come back. Yes I shall. I shall come back and fetch you as soon as I can. Of course I will.'

But Hedley, who knew better, shook his head solemnly and held his tears right on the brim until later.

Didge was halfway down the stairs when he thought of Daddo. If he was asleep he could just look in and then go. That would be best. And if he was still awake he'd have to make sure he didn't put his lamp on. Daddo had never liked women in pink. He listened at the door with Hedley pulling on his jacket and rolling his eyes.

'I'm coming, Hed. Just a minute. I can't flit without putting my head round the door.'

Daddo seemed to be having another of his nightmares. He was breathless and frantic, and with the landing light behind him it looked to Didge as though Daddo had surprised a crazed intruder. He was astride it, sweat glistening on his back. His pyjama trousers had been ripped off in the struggle and it sounded as though he had the better of it for the body beneath him was gasping and desperate.

'Oh God . . . Oh God. All right . . . All right. Oh God!'

Hedley placed himself between Didge and the bed and thrust his fat little hands up to cover Didge's eyeballs. But Didge had already switched on the overhead light and could see through Hedley's fishy fingers that Daddo was sporting a Stallion Tickler and was going at it hammer and tongs with a flushed and exhausted woman.

156

'Hello, Didge.' Her hair had grown longer, and her belly was swollen with child. But there could be no mistake. It was Kerry-Gene.

Daddo came to the point and blew his nose.

'Hello, son. I've been meaning to ask how you'd feel about a baby brother.'

'I've got to go. I'm in a hurry. I've told Hedley to behave himself and now I'm telling you. I don't want to come back and find this place knee-deep in toddle-trucks. And be careful.'

'You don't mind then, son?'

'What?'

'About Kerry-Gene.'

'Mind? I send her out for a video cassette and six months later she's still not turned up with it. And you, you bastard. I've asked you and asked you where my "Living Planet" tape was. And all the while it was up here. I'm furious.'

'Have a nice time, son.'

'And you just watch your bloody step. I've got problems enough without you. Have you ever tried walking in women's shoes?'

'All right then, son. Mind how you go.'

Didge turned away pushing Hedley in front of him.

'And, son?'

'Yes?'

'You've got a snag in them tights already.'

Didge banged the door so hard it sprang open again, and ran downstairs to find the shoes.

Hedley did the signal. The hall light was to go on and off once. They were to count to twenty. And then it would be time for Didge to go over the top. As they reached the count of ten and opened the door a crack, the night was filled with the sound of drums and wailing. From each end of the street a solid front of wimmin was advancing on the beleaguered men. They had painted their faces and teased their hair. They had taken up cudgels. Found their voices. Got in touch with their

157

anger. And in the heart of the ManPower contingent, surrounded by his standard-bearers, Corrigan cursed and felt the fluttering in his bowel grow unmanageable.

Didge ran for it, wide-legged and sway-backed. His first outing in heels. At the end of the street Bella was holding the car door open for him, her right foot cautioning the accelerator pedal. He locked himself in and they looked back for a moment. The banner was raised briefly. It said 'Onward and Upward With Didge'. It went down under the second wave of womanry.

As Bella turned out of the road and put her foot down, they ran into another faction, shoulder to shoulder blocking the way. Not wimmin. Not ManPower. A different lot. With flaming torches. Bella wound her window down a fraction.

'Would you please clear the road and let us through.'

'What's your business, Sister?'

'None of yours, sunshine. Now clear the road and let us through.'

'Not until we have found Him.'

'Who are you looking for?'

'He who bears The Mark. He who has brought us The Sign.'

A large man stepped out of the torchlight. He had a pig on a rope. He squashed his face to the opening in Bella's window and asked her straight,

'Are you hiding anything in your life, Sister?' It was Praise The Lord Logan. He didn't notice Didge.

'No, Brother. Not a thing. But I'd like to be moving on if you and your pig would kindly step to one side.'

'Have you seen him?'

'Who?'

'The Blessed One Who Has Come.'

'Who?'

'Our Blessed One. The One they call Didge.'

Didge leaned across.

'He lives down there on the right. It's the house with the

158

privet hedge and the thronging multitude outside. You can't miss it.'

Bella kicked him.

'Bless you, Sister. Bless you for guiding us to Him.'

'Who is it that wants him?'

'He will know us when He sees us. He is waiting for us.'

'Well I hope he's got some extra milk in. There's quite a lot of you.'

'Didge be with you, Sister.'

'And Didge be with you. What's the pig for?'

'That's for the triumphal journey.'

'A Pig Roast?'

'Brother Swills has given his pig for the triumphal return to Thrapston. The beast will carry Him in triumph.'

'The pig is to carry Didge?'

'In triumph.'

'I've heard he's quite a big man. Haven't you anything stronger?'

'We couldn't get Brother Ratcliffe's donkey started.'

Didge thought hard about not laughing before he risked using his voice: 'Well I think you'll have trouble with a pig. The only thing is, I've heard that the one they call Didge has been seen to levitate.'

Bella kicked him again.

Brother Logan passed the word back and it travelled quickly mouth to ear that the Blessed Didge could now almost certainly fly and would travel back to Thrapston supported only by angels. The cry went up 'Praise the Lord, Praise the Lord', and the brethren made a way through so that Bella could edge the car forward. And the last thing Didge saw was Glenda dragging two limp men into her garden, and Logan, with biscuits, coaxing the pig to take a few more steps.

They headed straight for the station.

'And who were they?'

'They, Filbert, were the Really Born Again This Time Christians.'

'And what did they want with me?'

'Charisma, darling.'

'Sorry?'

'They just want a little charismatic leadership. Someone to stand on a box and say things. Someone to ride in triumph on a pig, and then end up boiled in oil for the salvation of all mankind.'

'But ManPower wanted me.'

'Well there you are. Qualities of leadership are hard to find these days. I'm sorry about the clothes by the way.'

'I think Hedley did well. The tights are a bit of a trial, but I love the jacket.'

'Dear Hedley. He did get carried away. But you make a good woman. I can quite believe in you. Can I borrow your jacket some time?'

Didge didn't answer.

'Are you all right? It's been such a rush.'

'Daddo was doing something with Kerry-Gene. I thought I'd lost her. He was behaving very badly. For his age.'

'He's younger than me.'

'You don't behave badly.'

'Filbert! No wonder the Really Born Agains want you. I behave badly as often as possible. I waited for years for Ros to do it. Gave her every chance. With a bishop for a father I had every confidence in her. And when she wouldn't, I resolved that I would. Are you ready to jump out?'

'I owe you for the clothes.'

'You owe me nothing. What do you think you'll do?'

'I might learn to drive a car. When shall I see you again?'

'I don't know, Filbert. I'm an old girl and there's a lot left to be done. I'd like to keep an eye on Hedley though. He's a precious boy.'

160

She pulled into the station forecourt and left the engine running.

'On your way then! Travel safely.' She tucked some coins into his jacket pocket.

'I can't take that, Bella.'

'Take it. See if you can use it for your ticket. I think they'll take cash.'

'But I've got my plastic with me.'

'Take it! It's the last thing I can do for you. Where will you go?'

'I thought you'd be going to tell me.'

'No. I'll make a suggestion.'

'Yes?'

'Scotland would be safe.'

Didge pulled a face.

'I know, I know . . . But it would be safe. That's all.'

'What about ManPower? Don't they have that up there?'

'Shouldn't think so. Shouldn't think there's any need. Women up there locked themselves up and threw away the key years ago. There'll be something else. Sure to be. Wherever you go there'll be something. Give it a try. You might like it.'

'I'll keep in touch.'

'Be careful.'

'I'll come back to see you when this is all over.'

'If you say so, Filbert.'

'Goodbye, Bella. I hope Ros shows up.'

'Filbert! Go away!'

He walked away from the little car, unsteady on his heels, ill at ease with his hands. Bella wound down her window and called after him.

'Remember, Scotland would be sensible. And, Filbert, keep your knees together.'

A threat of violence unbecoming of a middle-aged lady in dusk rose sunray pleats, elicited the information that the slow train

161

to Edinburgh Waverley might stop at Kettering some time after midnight. Didge let the startled man drop back into his seat but held on to his Britrail tie until he was safely booked onto the night train west out of Paddington and the morning boat to Rosslare.

The clerk ran a finger right round the inside of his collar and enjoyed the feeling of space. He slammed down his shatter-proof security window and murmured that a woman of her age should be ashamed.

Didge pressed his shiny nose to the Speak Here holes and raised his voice an octave.

'A woman of my age? A woman of my age? Listen, you state-owned pile of excrement! A woman of my age is a thing of beauty and a joy forever!' And he flounced away to catch the London train, stopping at Wellingborough and Luton only. But he found it very difficult to keep his knees together.